The Beatrix Potter
Collection
Volume Two

THE BEATRIX POTTER COLLECTION

VOLUME TWO

WORDSWORTH CLASSICS

For my husband
ANTHONY JOHN RANSON
with love from your wife, the publisher.
Eternally grateful for your unconditional love.

Readers who are interested in other titles from
Wordsworth Editions are invited to visit our website at
www.wordsworth-editions.com

First published in 2014 by Wordsworth Editions Limited
8B East Street, Ware, Hertfordshire SG12 9HJ

ISBN   978 1 84022 724 6

Text copyright © Wordsworth Editions Limited 2014

Wordsworth® is a registered trade mark of
Wordsworth Editions Limited

Wordsworth Editions
is the company founded in 1987 by
MICHAEL TRAYLER

Typeset in Great Britain by Antony Gray
Printed and bound by Clays Ltd, St Ives plc

IN THIS BOOK

The Tale of Mrs Tiggy-Winkle

To the real little Lucie of Newlands

ONCE upon a time there was a little girl called Lucie, who lived at a farm called Littletown. She was a good little girl – only she was always losing her pocket-handkerchiefs!

One day little Lucie came into the farmyard crying – oh, she did cry so! 'I've lost my pocket-handkin! Three handkins and a pinny! Have *you* seen them, Tabby Kitten?'

The kitten went on washing her white paws; so Lucie asked a speckled hen –

'Sally Henny-penny, have *you* found three pocket-handkins?'

But the speckled hen ran into a barn, clucking, 'I go barefoot, barefoot, barefoot!'

And then Lucie asked Cock Robin sitting on a twig. Cock Robin looked sideways at Lucie with his bright black eye, then he flew over a stile and away.

Lucie climbed upon the stile and looked up at the hill behind Little-town — a hill that goes up — up — into the clouds as though it had no top!

And a great way up the hillside she thought she saw some white things spread upon the grass.

The Tale of Mrs Tiggy-Winkle

Lucie scrambled up the hill as fast as her short legs would carry her; she ran along a steep pathway — up and up — until Littletown was right away down below — she could have dropped a pebble down the chimney!

Presently she came to a spring, bubbling out from the hillside.

Someone had stood a tin can upon a stone to catch the water – but the water was already running over, for the can was no bigger than an egg-cup! And where the sand upon the path was wet there were footmarks of a *very* small person.

Lucie ran on, and on.

The path ended under a big rock. The grass was short and green, and there were clothes-props cut from bracken stems,

with lines of plaited rushes, and a heap of tiny clothes pins — but no pocket-handkerchiefs!

But there was something else — a door! straight into the hill; and inside it some-one was singing —

> 'Lily-white and clean, oh!
> With little frills between, oh!
> Smooth and hot — red rusty spot
> Never here be seen, oh!'

Lucie knocked – once – twice, and interrupted the song. A little frightened voice called out, 'Who's that?'

Lucie opened the door: and what do you think there was inside the hill? – a

nice clean kitchen with a flagged floor
and wooden beams — just like any other
farm kitchen. Only the ceiling was so
low that Lucie's head nearly touched it;
and the pots and pans were small, and so
was everything there.

There was a nice hot singey smell; and at the table, with an iron in her hand, stood a very stout short person staring anxiously at Lucie.

Her print gown was tucked up, and she was wearing a large apron over her striped petticoat. Her little black nose went sniffle, sniffle, snuffle, and her eyes went twinkle, twinkle; and underneath her cap – where Lucie had yellow curls – that little person had *prickles*!

'Who are you?' said Lucie. 'Have you seen my pocket-handkins?'

The little person made a bob-curtsey — 'Oh yes, if you please'm; my name is Mrs Tiggy-Winkle; oh yes if you please'm, I'm an excellent clear-starcher!' And she took something out of the clothes basket, and spread it on the ironing-blanket.

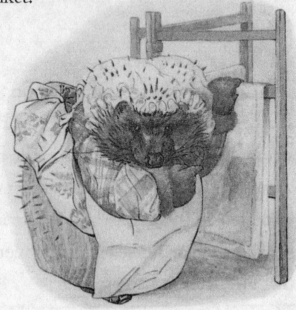

'What's that thing?' said Lucie — 'that's not my pocket-handkin?'

'Oh no, if you please'm; that's a little scarlet waistcoat belonging to Cock Robin!'

And she ironed it and folded it, and put it on one side.

Then she took something else off a clothes-horse — 'That isn't my pinny?' said Lucie.

'Oh no, if you please'm; that's a damask tablecloth belonging to Jenny Wren; look how it's stained with currant wine! It's very bad to wash!' said Mrs Tiggy-Winkle.

Mrs Tiggy-Winkle's nose went sniffle, sniffle, snuffle, and her eyes went twinkle, twinkle; and she fetched another hot iron from the fire.

'There's one of my pocket-handkins!' cried Lucie – 'and there's my pinny!'

Mrs Tiggy-Winkle ironed it, and goffered it, and shook out the frills.

'Oh, that *is* lovely!' said Lucie.

'And what are those long yellow things with fingers like gloves?'

'Oh that's a pair of stockings belonging to Sally Henny-Penny – look how she's worn the heels out with scratching in the yard! She'll very soon go barefoot!' said Mrs Tiggy-Winkle.

'Why, there's another hankersniff —
but it isn't mine; it's red.'

'Oh no, if you please'm; that one
belongs to old Mrs Rabbit; and it *did* so
smell of onions! I've had to wash it
separately. I can't get out that smell.'

'There's another one of mine,' said Lucie. 'What are those funny little white things?'

'That's a pair of mittens belonging to Tabby Kitten; I only have to iron them; she washes them herself.'

'There's my last pocket-handkin!' said Lucie. 'And what are you dipping into the basin of starch?'

The Tale of Mrs Tiggy-Winkle

'They're little dicky shirt-fronts belonging to Tom Titmouse — most terrible particular!' said Mrs Tiggy-Winkle. 'Now I've finished my ironing, I'm going to air some clothes.'

'What are these dear soft fluffy things?' said Lucie.

'Oh, those are woolly coats belonging to the little lambs at Skelghyl.'

'Will their jackets take off?' asked Lucie.

'Oh yes, if you please'm; look at the sheep-mark on the shoulder. And here's one marked for Gatesgarth, and three

The Tale of Mrs Tiggy-Winkle

that come from Littletown. They're *always* marked at washing!' said Mrs Tiggy-Winkle.

And she hung up all sorts and sizes of clothes – small brown coats of mice; and one velvety black moleskin waistcoat;

and a red tail-coat with no tail belonging to Squirrel Nutkin; and a very much shrunk blue jacket belonging to Peter Rabbit; and a petticoat, not marked, that had gone lost in the washing — and at last the basket was empty!

Then Mrs Tiggy-Winkle made tea — a cup for herself and a cup for Lucie. They sat before the fire on a bench and looked sideways at one another. Mrs Tiggy-Winkle's hand, holding the teacup, was very, very brown and very, very wrinkly with the soapsuds; and all through her gown and her cap, there were *hairpins* sticking wrong end out, so that Lucie didn't like to sit too near her.

When they had finished tea, they tied up the clothes in bundles; and Lucie's

The Tale of Mrs Tiggy-Winkle

pocket-handkerchiefs were folded up inside her clean pinny and fastened with a silver safety-pin.

And then they made up the fire with turf, and came out and locked the door, and hid the key under the door-sill.

Then away down the hill trotted Lucie and Mrs Tiggy-Winkle with the bundles of clothes!

All the way down the path little
animals came out of the fern to meet
them; the very first that they met were
Peter Rabbit and Benjamin Bunny!

And she gave them their nice clean clothes; and all the little animals and birds were so very much obliged to dear Mrs Tiggy-Winkle.

So that at the bottom of the hill when they came to the stile, there was nothing left to carry except Lucie's one little bundle.

Lucie scrambled up the stile with the bundle in her hand; and then she turned to say, 'Good-night,' and to thank the washerwoman. But what a *very* odd thing!

Mrs Tiggy-Winkle had not waited either
for thanks or for the washing bill!

She was running, running, running up
the hill – and where was her white frilled
cap? and her shawl? and her gown? and
her petticoat?

And *how* small she had grown – and *how* brown – and covered with *prickles!*

Why! Mrs Tiggy-Winkle was nothing but a *hedgehog!*

✳   ✳   ✳

(Now some people say that little Lucie had been asleep upon the stile – but then how could she have found three clean pocket-handkins and a pinny, pinned with a silver safety-pin?

And besides – *I* have seen that door into the back of the hill called Cat Bells – and am very well acquainted with dear Mrs Tiggy-Winkle!)

The Tale of Samuel Whiskers

or the Roly-Poly Pudding

In remembrance of 'Sammy',
the intelligent pink-eyed
representative of a persecuted
(but irrepressible) race,
an affectionate little friend
and most accomplished thief!

Once upon a time there was an old cat, called Mrs Tabitha Twitchit, who was an anxious parent. She used to lose her kittens continually, and whenever they were lost they were always in mischief!

On baking day she determined to shut them up in a cupboard.

She caught Moppet and Mittens, but she could not find Tom.

Mrs Tabitha went up and down all over the house, mewing for Tom Kitten. She looked in the pantry under the staircase, and she searched the best spare bedroom that was all covered up with dust sheets. She went right upstairs and looked into the attics, but she could not find him anywhere.

It was an old, old house, full of cupboards and passages. Some of the walls were four feet thick, and there used to be queer noises inside them, as if there might be a little secret staircase. Certainly there were odd little jagged doorways in the wainscot, and things disappeared at night — especially cheese and bacon.

Mrs Tabitha became more and more distracted and mewed dreadfully.

The Tale of Samuel Whiskers

While their mother was searching the house, Moppet and Mittens had got into mischief.

The
cupboard
door was
not locked,
so they
pushed it open and came out.
They went straight to the dough which
was set to rise in a pan before the fire.

They patted
it with their
little soft
paws –
'Shall we
make dear little

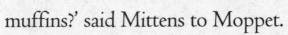

muffins?' said Mittens to Moppet.

But just at that moment somebody
knocked at the front-door, and Moppet
jumped into the flour barrel in a fright.

Mittens ran away to the dairy and hid in an empty jar on the stone shelf where the milk pans stand.

The visitor was a neighbour, Mrs Ribby; she had called to borrow some yeast.

Mrs Tabitha came downstairs mewing dreadfully – 'Come in, Cousin Ribby, come in, and sit ye down! I'm in sad trouble, Cousin Ribby,' said

Tabitha, shedding tears. 'I've lost my dear son Thomas; I'm afraid the rats have got him.' She wiped her eyes with her apron.

'He's a bad kitten, Cousin Tabitha; he made a cat's cradle of my best bonnet last time I came to tea. Where have you looked for him?'

'All over the house! The rats are too many for me. What a thing it is to have an unruly family!' said Mrs Tabitha Twitchit.

'I'm not afraid of rats; I will help you to find him — and whip him, too! What is all that soot in the fender?'

'The chimney wants sweeping. Oh, dear me, Cousin Ribby – now Moppet and Mittens are gone! They have both got out of the cupboard!'

Ribby and Tabitha set to work to search the house thoroughly again. They poked under the beds with Ribby's umbrella and they rummaged in cupboards. They even fetched a candle and looked inside a clothes chest in one of the attics. They could not find anything,

but once they heard a door bang and somebody scuttered downstairs.

'Yes, it is infested with rats,' said Tabitha tearfully. 'I caught seven young

ones out of one hole in the back kitchen, and we had them for dinner last Saturday. And once I saw the old father rat – an enormous old rat – Cousin Ribby. I was just going to jump upon him, when he showed his yellow teeth at me and whisked down the hole. These rats get upon my nerves so, Cousin Ribby,' said Tabitha.

Ribby and Tabitha searched and searched. They both heard a curious roly-poly noise under the attic floor. But there was nothing to be seen.

They returned to the kitchen. 'Here's one of your kittens at least,' said Ribby, dragging Moppet out of the flour barrel.

They shook the flour off her and set her down on the kitchen floor. She seemed to be in a terrible fright.

'Oh! mother, mother,' said Moppet, 'there's been an old woman rat in the kitchen, and she's stolen some of the dough!'

The two cats ran to look at the dough pan. Sure enough there were marks of little scratching fingers, and a lump of dough was gone!

'Which way did she go, Moppet?'

But Moppet had been too much frightened to peep out of the barrel again.

Ribby and Tabitha took her with

them to keep her safely in sight while they went on with their search.

They went into the dairy.

The first thing they found was Mittens, hiding in an empty jar.

They tipped over the jar, and she scrambled out.

'Oh, mother, mother!' said Mittens — 'Oh! mother, mother, there has been an old man rat in the dairy — a dreadful

'normous big rat, mother; and he's stolen a pat of butter and the rolling pin.'

Ribby and Tabitha looked at one another.

'A rolling pin and butter! Oh, my poor son Thomas!' exclaimed Tabitha, wringing her paws.

'A rolling pin?' said Ribby. 'Did we not hear a roly-poly noise in the attic when we were looking into that chest?'

Ribby and Tabitha rushed upstairs
again. Sure enough the roly-poly noise
was still going on quite distinctly under
the attic floor.

'This is serious, Cousin Tabitha,' said
Ribby. 'We must send for John Joiner at
once, with a saw.'

*　　*　　*

Now, this is what had been happening to Tom Kitten, and it shows how very unwise it is to go up a chimney in a very old house, where a person does not know his way and where there are enormous rats.

Tom Kitten did not want to be shut up in a cupboard. When he saw that his mother was going to bake, he determined to hide.

The Tale of Samuel Whiskers

He looked about for a nice convenient
place, and he fixed upon the chimney.

The fire had only just been lighted,

and it was not hot; but there was a white choky smoke from the green sticks. Tom Kitten got up on the fender and looked up. It was a big old-fashioned fireplace.

The chimney itself was wide enough inside for a man to stand up and walk about. So there was plenty of room for a little Tom Cat.

He jumped right up into the fireplace,

balancing himself upon the iron bar where the kettle hangs.

Tom Kitten took another big jump off the bar and landed on a ledge high up inside the chimney, knocking down some soot into the fender.

Tom Kitten coughed and choked with the smoke; he could hear the sticks beginning to crackle and burn in the fireplace down below. He made up his mind to climb right to the top, and get out on to the slates, and try to catch sparrows.

'I cannot go back. If I slipped I might fall into the fire and singe my beautiful tail and my little blue jacket.'

The chimney was a very big old-fashioned one. It was built in the days when people burnt logs of wood upon the hearth.

The chimney stack stood up above the roof like a little stone tower, and the daylight shone down from the top, under the slanting slates that kept out the rain.

Tom Kitten was getting very frightened! He climbed up, and up, and up.

Then he waded sideways through inches of soot. He was like a little sweep himself.

It was most confusing in the dark. One flue seemed to lead into another.

There was less smoke, but Tom Kitten felt quite lost.

He scrambled up and up; but before he reached the chimney top he came to

a place where somebody had loosened a stone in the wall. There were some mutton bones lying about.

'This seems funny,' said Tom Kitten. 'Who has been gnawing bones up here in the chimney? I wish I had never come! And what a funny smell? It is something like mouse, only dreadfully strong. It makes me sneeze,' said Tom Kitten.

He squeezed through the hole in the wall and dragged himself along a most uncomfortably tight passage where there was scarcely any light.

He groped his way carefully for several
yards; he was at the back of the skirting
board in the attic, where there is a little
mark * in the picture.

All at once, in the dark, he fell head
over heels down a hole, and landed on a
heap of very dirty rags.

When Tom Kitten picked himself up
and looked about him, he found himself
in a place that he had never seen before,
although he had lived all his life in the

house. It was a very small, stuffy, fusty room, with boards, and rafters, and cobwebs, and lath and plaster.

Opposite to him — as far away as he could sit — was an enormous rat.

'What do you mean by tumbling into my bed all covered with smuts?' said the rat, chattering his teeth.

'Please, sir, the chimney wants sweeping,' said poor Tom Kitten.

'Anna Maria! Anna Maria!' squeaked the rat. There was a pattering noise and an old woman rat poked her head round a rafter.

All in a minute she rushed upon Tom Kitten, and before he knew what was happening...

...his coat was pulled off, and he was

rolled up in a bundle, and tied with string in very hard knots.

Anna Maria did the tying. The old rat watched her and took snuff. When she had finished, they both sat staring at him with their mouths open.

'Anna Maria,' said the old man rat (whose name was Samuel Whiskers),

'Anna Maria, make me a kitten-dumpling roly-poly pudding for my dinner.'

'It requires dough and a pat of butter and a rolling pin,' said Anna Maria, considering Tom Kitten with her head on one side.

'No,' said Samuel Whiskers, 'make it properly, Anna Maria, with bread-crumbs.'

'Nonsense! Butter and dough,' replied Anna Maria.

The two rats consulted together for a few minutes and then went away.

Samuel Whiskers got through a hole in the wainscot and went boldly down the front staircase to the dairy to get the butter. He did not meet anybody.

He made a second journey for the rolling pin. He pushed it in front of him with his paws, like a brewer's man trundling a barrel.

The Tale of Samuel Whiskers

He could hear Ribby and Tabitha talking, but they were too busy lighting the candle to look into the chest.

They did not see him.

Anna Maria went down by way of the skirting board and a window shutter to the kitchen to steal the dough.

She borrowed a small saucer and scooped up the dough with her paws.

She did not observe Moppet.

While Tom Kitten was left alone under the floor of the attic, he wriggled about and tried to mew for help.

But his mouth was full of soot and cobwebs, and he was tied up in such very tight knots, he could not make anybody hear him — except a spider who came out of a crack in the ceiling and examined the knots critically, from a safe distance.

It was a judge of knots because it had

a habit of tying up unfortunate blue-bottles. It did not offer to assist him.

Tom Kitten wriggled and squirmed until he was quite exhausted.

Presently the rats came back and set to work to make him into a dumpling. First they smeared him with butter and then they rolled him in the dough.

'Will not the string be very indigestible, Anna Maria?' enquired Samuel Whiskers.

Anna Maria said she thought that it was of no consequence; but she wished that Tom Kitten would hold his head still, as it disarranged the pastry. She laid hold of his ears.

Tom Kitten bit and spat, and mewed and wriggled; and the rolling pin went roly-poly, roly; roly-poly, roly. The rats each held an end.

'His tail is sticking out! You did not fetch enough dough, Anna Maria.'

'I fetched as much as I could carry,' replied Anna Maria.

'I do not think' — said Samuel Whiskers, pausing to take a look at Tom Kitten — 'I do *not* think it will be a good pudding. It smells sooty.'

Anna Maria was about to argue the point when all at once there began to be other sounds up above — the rasping noise of a saw, and the noise of a little dog, scratching and yelping!

The rats dropped the rolling pin and listened attentively.

'We are discovered and interrupted, Anna Maria; let us collect our property — and other people's — and depart at once.

'I fear that we shall be obliged to leave this pudding.

'But I am persuaded that the knots would have proved indigestible, whatever you may urge to the contrary.'

'Come away at once and help me to tie up some mutton bones in a counterpane,' said Anna Maria. 'I have got half a smoked ham hidden in the chimney.'

So it happened that by the time

John Joiner had got the plank up there was nobody under the floor except the rolling pin and Tom Kitten in a very dirty dumpling!

But there was a strong smell of rats; and John Joiner spent the rest of the morning

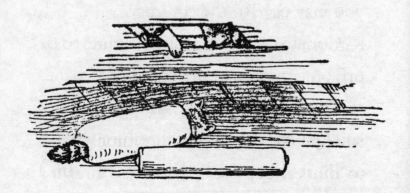

sniffing and whining and wagging his tail and going round and round with his head in the hole like a gimlet.

Then he nailed the plank down again and put his tools in his bag and came downstairs.

The cat family had quite recovered. They invited him to stay to dinner.

The dumpling had been peeled off Tom Kitten and made separately into a bag pudding, with currants in it to hide the smuts.

They had been obliged to put Tom Kitten into a hot bath to get the butter off.

John Joiner smelt the pudding; but he regretted that he had not time to stay to dinner, because he had just finished

making a wheelbarrow for Miss Potter, and she had ordered two hen coops.

And when I was going to the post late in the afternoon — I looked up the lane from the corner, and I saw Mr Samuel Whiskers and his wife on the run, with big bundles on a little wheelbarrow, which looked very much like mine.

They were just turning in at the gate to the barn of Farmer Potatoes.

Samuel Whiskers was puffing and out of breath. Anna Maria was still arguing in shrill tones.

She seemed to know her way, and she seemed to have a quantity of luggage.

I am sure *I* never gave her leave to borrow my wheelbarrow!

They went into the barn and hauled their parcels with a bit of string to the top of the haymow.

After that, there were no more rats for a long time at Tabitha Twitchit's.

As for Farmer Potatoes, he has been driven nearly distracted. There are rats, and rats, and rats in his barn! They eat up the chicken food, and steal the oats and bran, and make holes in the meal bags.

And they are all descended from Mr and Mrs Samuel Whiskers – children and grandchildren and great-great-grand-children. There is no end to them!

Moppet and Mittens have grown up into very good rat-catchers.

They go out rat-catching in the village, and they find plenty of employment. They charge so much a dozen and earn their living very comfortably.

They hang up the rats' tails in a row on the barn door, to show how many they have caught — dozens and dozens of them.

But Tom Kitten has always been afraid of a rat; he never durst face anything that is bigger than –

a mouse.

The Tale of the Flopsy Bunnies

To all little friends of
Mr McGregor and
Peter and Benjamin

It is said that the effect of eating too much lettuce is 'soporific'.

I have never felt sleepy after eating lettuces; but then *I* am not a rabbit.

They certainly had a very soporific effect upon the Flopsy Bunnies!

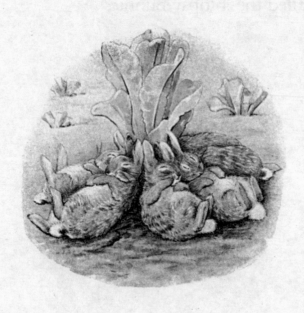

When Benjamin Bunny grew up, he married his Cousin Flopsy. They had a large family, and they were very improvident and cheerful.

I do not remember the separate names of their children; they were generally called the 'Flopsy Bunnies'.

The Tale of the Flopsy Bunnies

As there was not always quite enough to eat, Benjamin used to borrow cabbages from Flopsy's brother, Peter Rabbit, who kept a nursery garden.

Sometimes Peter Rabbit had no cabbages to spare.

The Tale of the Flopsy Bunnies

When this happened, the Flopsy Bunnies went across the field to a rubbish heap, in the ditch outside Mr McGregor's garden.

Mr McGregor's rubbish heap was a mixture. There were jam pots and paper bags, and mountains of chopped grass from the mowing machine (which always tasted oily), and some rotten vegetable marrows and an old boot or two. One day – oh, joy! – there was a quantity of overgrown lettuces, which had 'shot' into flower.

The Tale of the Flopsy Bunnies

The Flopsy Bunnies simply stuffed themselves with lettuces. By degrees, one after another, they were overcome with slumber and lay down in the mown grass.

Benjamin was not so much overcome as his children. Before going to sleep he was sufficiently wide awake to put a paper bag over his head to keep off the flies.

The little Flopsy Bunnies slept delightfully in the warm sun. From the lawn beyond the garden came the distant clacketty sound of the mowing machine. The bluebottles buzzed about the wall, and a little old mouse picked over the rubbish among the jam pots.

(I can tell you her name — she was called Thomasina Tittlemouse, and she was a woodmouse with a long tail.)

She rustled across the paper bag, and awakened Benjamin Bunny.

The mouse apologised profusely, and said that she knew Peter Rabbit.

While she and Benjamin were talking, close under the wall, they heard a heavy tread above their heads; and suddenly Mr McGregor emptied out a sackful of lawn mowings right upon the top of the sleeping Flopsy Bunnies! Benjamin shrank down under his paper bag. The mouse hid in a jam pot.

The Tale of the Flopsy Bunnies

The little rabbits smiled sweetly in their sleep under the shower of grass; they did not awake because the lettuces had been so soporific.

They dreamt that their mother Flopsy was tucking them up in a hay bed.

Mr McGregor looked down after emptying his sack. He saw some funny little brown tips of ears sticking up through the lawn mowings. He stared at them for some time.

Presently a fly settled on one of them and it moved.

Mr McGregor climbed down on to the rubbish heap –

'One, two, three, four, five, six leetle rabbits!' said he as he dropped them into his sack. The Flopsy Bunnies dreamt that their mother was turning them over in bed. They stirred a little in their sleep, but still they did not wake up.

Mr McGregor tied up the sack and left it on the wall.

He went to put away the mowing machine.

While he was gone, Mrs Flopsy Bunny (who had remained at home) came across the field.

She looked suspiciously at the sack and wondered where everybody was?

The Tale of the Flopsy Bunnies

Then the mouse came out of her jam
pot, and Benjamin took the paper bag off
his head, and they told the doleful tale.

Benjamin and Flopsy were in despair,
they could not undo the string.

But Mrs Tittlemouse was a resourceful

person. She nibbled a hole in the bottom corner of the sack.

The little rabbits were pulled out and pinched to wake them.

Their parents stuffed the empty sack with three rotten vegetable marrows, an

old blacking brush and two decayed turnips.

Then they all hid under a bush and watched for Mr McGregor.

Mr McGregor came back and picked up the sack and carried it off.

He carried it hanging down, as if it were rather heavy.

The Tale of the Flopsy Bunnies

The Flopsy Bunnies followed at a safe distance.

They watched him go into his house. And then they crept up to the window to listen.

Mr McGregor threw down the sack on the stone floor in a way that would have been extremely painful to the Flopsy Bunnies if they had happened to be inside it.

They could hear him drag his chair on the flags, and chuckle.

'One, two, three, four, five, six leetle rabbits!' said Mr McGregor. 'Eh? What's that? What have they been

spoiling now?'
enquired
Mrs
McGregor.
'One, two,
three, four,
five, six
leetle fat
rabbits!'
repeated
Mr McGregor, counting on his fingers –
'One, two, three –'

'Don't you be silly: what do you mean,
you silly old man?'

'In the sack! one, two, three, four, five,
six!' replied Mr McGregor.

(The youngest Flopsy Bunny got up
on the windowsill.)

Mrs McGregor took hold of the sack and felt it. She said she could feel six, but they must be *old* rabbits, because they were so hard and all different shapes.

'Not fit to eat; but the skins will do fine to line my old cloak.'

'Line your old cloak?' shouted Mr McGregor – 'I shall sell them and buy myself baccy!'

'Rabbit tobacco! I shall skin them and cut off their heads.'

Mrs McGregor untied the sack and put her hand inside.

When she felt the vegetables she became very, very angry. She said that Mr McGregor had 'done it a purpose'.

And Mr McGregor was very angry too. One of the rotten marrows came flying through the kitchen window, and hit the youngest Flopsy Bunny.

He was rather hurt.

Then Benjamin and Flopsy thought that it was time to go home.

So Mr McGregor did not get his tobacco, and Mrs McGregor did not get her rabbit skins.

But next Christmas Thomasina Tittle-mouse got a present of enough rabbit wool to make herself a cloak and a hood, and a handsome muff and a pair of warm mittens.

The Tale of
Ginger and Pickles

With very kind regards to old
Mr John Taylor, who 'thinks he
might pass as a dormouse'!
(Three years in bed and
never a grumble!)

Once upon a time there was a village shop. The name over the window was 'Ginger and Pickles'.

It was a little small shop just the right size for dolls – Lucinda and Jane Doll-Cook always bought their groceries at Ginger and Pickles.

The counter inside was a convenient height for rabbits. Ginger and Pickles sold red spotty pocket handkerchiefs at a penny three farthings.

They also sold sugar and snuff and galoshes.

In fact, although it was such a small shop it sold nearly everything – except a few things that you want in a hurry – like bootlaces, hairpins and mutton chops.

Ginger and Pickles were the people who kept the shop. Ginger was a yellow tomcat and Pickles was a terrier.

The rabbits were always a little bit afraid of Pickles.

The shop was also patronised by mice – only the mice were rather afraid of Ginger.

The Tale of the Ginger and Pickles

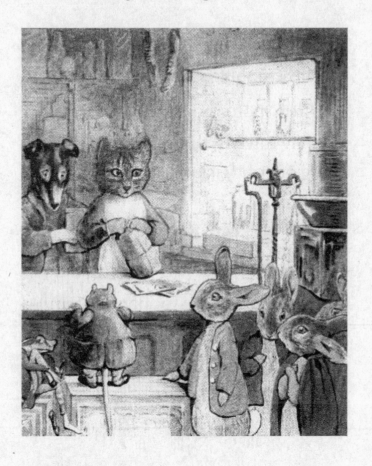

Ginger usually requested Pickles to serve them, because he said it made his mouth water.

'I cannot bear,' said he, 'to see them going out of the door carrying their little parcels.'

'I have the same feeling about rats,' replied Pickles, 'but it would never do to eat our customers; they would leave us and go to Tabitha Twitchit's.'

'On the contrary, they would go no-where,' replied Ginger gloomily.

(Tabitha Twitchit kept the only other shop in the village. She did not give credit.)

But there was no money in what was called the 'till'.

Ginger and Pickles gave unlimited credit.

Now the meaning of 'credit' was this — when a customer bought a bar of soap, instead of the customer pulling out a purse and paying for it, she said she would pay another time.

And Pickles made a low bow and said, 'With pleasure, madam,' and it was written down in a book.

The customers came again and again,

and bought quantities, in spite of being afraid of Ginger and Pickles.

The customers came in crowds every day and bought quantities, especially the toffee customers. But there was always no money; they never paid for as much as a pennyworth of peppermints.

But the sales were enormous, ten times as large as Tabitha Twitchit's.

As there was always no money, Ginger and Pickles were obliged to eat their own goods. Pickles ate biscuits and Ginger ate a dried haddock.

They ate them by candlelight after the shop was closed.

When it came to January the first there was still no money, and Pickles was unable to buy a dog licence.

'It is very unpleasant. I am afraid of the police,' said Pickles.

'It is your own fault for being a terrier; *I* do not require a licence, and neither does Kep, the collie dog.'

'It is very uncomfortable. I am afraid I shall be summoned. I have tried in vain to get a licence upon credit at the Post

Office;' said Pickles. 'The place is full of policemen. I met one as I was coming home.

'Let us send in the bill again to Samuel Whiskers, Ginger, he owes twenty-two shillings and ninepence for bacon.'

'I do not believe that he intends to pay at all,' replied Ginger.

'And I feel sure that Anna Maria pockets things – where are all the cream crackers?'

'You have eaten them yourself,' replied Ginger.

Ginger and Pickles retired into the back parlour. They did accounts. They added up sums and sums and sums.

'Samuel Whiskers has run up a bill as long as his tail; he has had an ounce and three-quarters of snuff since October!'

'What is seven pounds of butter at one shilling and threepence a pound, and a stick of sealing wax and four matches?'

'Send in all the bills again to everybody "with compliments",' suggested Ginger.

After a time they heard a noise in the shop, as if something had been pushed in at the door. They came out of the back parlour. There was an envelope lying on the counter, and a policeman writing in a notebook!

Pickles nearly had a fit, he barked and he barked and made little rushes.

'Bite him, Pickles! bite him!' spluttered

Ginger behind a sugar barrel. 'He's only a German doll!'

The policeman went on writing in his notebook; twice he put his pencil in his mouth, and once he dipped it in the treacle.

Pickles barked till he was hoarse. But still the policeman took no notice. He had bead eyes, and his helmet was sewn on with stitches.

At length, on his last little rush, Pickles found that the shop was empty. The policeman had disappeared.

But the envelope remained.

'Do you think that he has gone to fetch a real live policeman? I am afraid it is a summons,' said Pickles.

'No,' replied Ginger, who had opened the envelope, 'it is the rates and taxes — three pounds, nineteen shillings and elevenpence three farthings.'

'This is the last straw,' said Pickles, 'let us close the shop.'

They put up the shutters, and left.

But they have not removed from the neighbourhood. In fact some people wish they had gone farther.

Pickles is at present a gamekeeper.

Ginger is living in the warren. I do not know what occupation he pursues; he looks stout and comfortable.

The closing of the shop caused great inconvenience. Tabitha Twitchit immediately raised the price of everything by a halfpenny; and she continued to refuse to give credit.

Of course there were the tradesmen's carts — the butcher, the fishman and Timothy Baker.

But a person could not live on 'seed wigs' and sponge cake and butter buns — not even when the sponge cake was as good as Timothy's!

After a time Mr John Dormouse and his daughter began to sell peppermints and candles.

But they did not keep 'self-fitting sixes';

The Tale of the Ginger and Pickles

and it took five mice to carry one seven-inch candle.

Besides — the candles which they sold behaved very strangely in warm weather.

And Miss Dormouse refused to take back the ends when they were brought back to her with complaints.

And when Mr John Dormouse was complained to, he stayed in bed and

would say nothing but 'very snug'; which is not the way to carry on a retail business.

So everybody was pleased when Sally Henny Penny sent out a printed poster to say that she was going to reopen the shop: 'Henny's Opening Sale! Grand cooperative jumble! Penny's penny prices! Come buy, come try, come buy!'

The poster really was most 'ticing.

There was a rush upon the opening day. The shop was crammed with customers, and there were crowds of mice upon the biscuit cannisters.

The Tale of the Ginger and Pickles

Sally Henny Penny gets rather flustered when she tries to count out change – she insists on being paid cash; but she is quite harmless.

And she has laid in a remarkable assortment of bargains.

There is something to please everybody.

The Tale of
Mrs Tittlemouse

Nellie's little book

Once upon a time there was a woodmouse, and her name was Mrs Tittlemouse.

She lived in a bank under a hedge.

Such a funny house! There were yards and yards of sandy passages leading to storerooms and nut cellars and seed cellars, all among the roots of the hedge.

The Tale of Mrs Tittlemouse

There was a kitchen, a parlour, a pantry and a larder.

Also, there was Mrs Tittlemouse's bedroom, where she slept in a little box bed!

Mrs Tittlemouse was a most terribly tidy particular little mouse, always sweeping and dusting the soft sandy floors.

Sometimes a beetle lost its way in the passages.

'Shuh! shuh! little dirty feet!' said Mrs Tittlemouse, clattering her dustpan.

The Tale of Mrs Tittlemouse

And one day a little old woman ran up
and down in a red spotty cloak.

'Your house is on fire, Mother Lady-
bird! Fly away home to your children!'

Another day, a big fat spider came in to shelter from the rain.

'Beg pardon, is this not Miss Muffet's?'

'Go away, you bold bad spider! Leaving ends of cobweb all over my nice clean house!'

The Tale of Mrs Tittlemouse

She bundled the spider out at a window.

He let himself down the hedge with a long thin bit of string.

Mrs Tittlemouse went on her way to a distant storeroom to fetch cherry-stones and thistledown seed for dinner.

All along the passage she sniffed, and looked at the floor.

'I smell a smell of honey; is it the cowslips outside in the hedge? I am sure I can see the marks of little dirty feet.'

Suddenly round a corner, she met

The Tale of Mrs Tittlemouse

Babbitty
Bumble.
'Zizz,
bizz,
bizzz!'
said the
bumble-
bee.
Mrs
Tittlemouse
looked at her
severely. She wished that she had a
broom. 'Good-day, Babbitty Bumble; I
should be glad to buy some beeswax.
But what are you doing down here? Why
do you always come in at a window, and
say, Zizz, bizz, bizzz?' Mrs Tittlemouse
began to get cross.

'Zizz, wizz, wizzz!' replied Babbitty Bumble in a peevish squeak. She sidled down a passage, and disappeared into a storeroom which had been used for acorns.

Mrs Tittlemouse had eaten the acorns before Christmas; the storeroom ought to have been empty.

But it was full of untidy dry moss.

Mrs Tittlemouse began to pull out the moss. Three or four other bees put their heads out, and buzzed fiercely.

'I am not in the habit of letting lodgings; this is an intrusion!' said Mrs Tittlemouse. 'I will have them turned out — '

'Buzz! Buzz! Buzzz!' —

The Tale of Mrs Tittlemouse

'I wonder who would help me?'

'Bizz, wizz, Wizzz!'

'I will not have Mr Jackson; he never
wipes his feet.'

Beatrix Potter

Mrs Tittlemouse decided to leave the bees till after dinner.

When she got back to the parlour, she heard someone coughing in a fat voice; and there sat Mr Jackson himself.

He was sitting all over a small rocking

chair, twiddling his thumbs and smiling, with his feet on the fender.

He lived in a drain below the hedge, in a very dirty wet ditch.

'How do you do, Mr Jackson? Deary me, you have got very wet!'

'Thank you, thank you, thank you, Mrs Tittlemouse! I'll sit awhile and dry myself,' said Mr Jackson.

He sat and smiled, and the water dripped off his coat tails. Mrs Tittlemouse went round with a mop.

He sat such a while that he had to be asked if he would take some dinner?

First she offered him cherry-stones. 'Thank you, thank you, Mrs Tittlemouse! No teeth, no teeth, no teeth!' said Mr Jackson.

He opened his mouth most unnecessarily wide; he certainly had not a tooth in his head.

Then she offered him thistledown
seed — 'Tiddly, widdly, widdly! Pouff,
pouff, puff.' said Mr Jackson. He blew
the thistledown all over the room.

'Thank you, thank you, thank you,
Mrs Tittlemouse! Now what I really,
really should like — would be a little dish
of honey!'

'I am afraid I have not got any, Mr Jackson!' said Mrs Tittlemouse.

'Tiddly, widdly, widdly, Mrs Tittle-mouse!' said the smiling Mr Jackson, 'I can *smell* it; that is why I came to call.'

Mr Jackson rose ponderously from the table, and began to look into the cup-boards.

Mrs Tittle-mouse followed him with a dish-cloth, to wipe his large wet  footmarks off the parlour floor.

The Tale of Mrs Tittlemouse

When he had convinced himself that there was no honey in the cupboards, he began to walk down the passage.

'Indeed, indeed, you will stick fast, Mr Jackson!'

'Tiddly, widdly, widdly, Mrs Tittle-mouse!'

First he squeezed into the pantry.

'Tiddly, widdly, widdly? No honey? No honey, Mrs Tittlemouse?'

There were three creepy-crawly people hiding in the plate rack. Two of them got away; but the littlest one he caught.

Then he squeezed into the larder. Miss Butterfly was tasting the sugar; but she flew away out of the window.

'Tiddly, widdly, widdly, Mrs Tittlemouse; you seem to have plenty of visitors!'

'And without any invitation!' said Mrs Thomasina Tittlemouse.

They went along the sandy passage —
'Tiddly, widdly — '

'Buzz! Wizz! Wizz!'

He met Babbitty round a corner, and
snapped her up, and put her down again.

'I do not like bumble bees. They are
all over bristles,' said Mr Jackson, wiping
his mouth with his coat sleeve.

'Get out, you nasty old toad!' shrieked
Babbitty Bumble.

'I shall go distracted!' scolded Mrs Tittlemouse.

She shut herself in the nut cellar while Mr Jackson pulled out the bees-nest. He seemed to have no objection to stings.

When Mrs Tittlemouse ventured to come out, everybody had gone away.

But the untidiness was something dreadful. 'Never did I see such a mess — smears of honey — and moss and thistledown – and marks of big and little dirty feet – all over my nice clean house!'

She gathered up the moss and the remains of the beeswax.

Then she went out and fetched some twigs, partially to close up the front door.

'I will make it too small for Mr Jackson!'

She fetched soft soap and a flannel and a new scrubbing brush from the storeroom. But she was too tired to do any more. First she fell asleep in her chair, and then she went to bed.

'Will it ever be tidy again?' said poor Mrs Tittlemouse.

Next morning she got up very early and began a spring cleaning which lasted a fortnight.

She swept, and scrubbed, and dusted; and she rubbed up the furniture with beeswax, and polished her little tin spoons.

The Tale of Mrs Tittlemouse

When it was all beautifully neat and clean, she gave a party to five other little mice, without Mr Jackson.

He smelt the party and came up the bank, but he could not squeeze in at the door.

So they handed him out acorn-cupfuls of honeydew through the window, and he was not at all offended.

He sat outside in the sun, and said — 'Tiddly, widdly, widdly! Your very good health, Mrs Tittlemouse!'

The Tale of
Timmy Tiptoes

For many unknown little friends,
including Monica

Once upon a time there was a little fat comfortable grey squirrel called Timmy Tiptoes. He had a nest thatched with leaves in the top of a tall tree; and he had a little squirrel wife called Goody.

Timmy Tiptoes sat out, enjoying the breeze; he whisked his tail and chuckled — 'Little wife Goody, the nuts are ripe; we must lay up a store for winter and spring.'

Goody Tiptoes was busy pushing moss under the thatch — 'The nest is so snug, we shall be sound asleep all winter.'

'Then we shall wake up all the thinner

when there is nothing to eat, in spring-time,' replied prudent Timothy.

The Tale of Timmy Tiptoes

When Timmy and Goody Tiptoes came to the nut thicket, they found other squirrels were there already.

Timmy took off his jacket and hung it on a twig; they worked away quietly by themselves.

Every day they made several journeys and picked quantities of nuts. They carried them away in bags, and stored them in several hollow stumps near the tree where they had built their nest.

The Tale of Timmy Tiptoes

When these
stumps were
full, they
began to
empty the
bags into a
hole high up
a tree that
had belonged
to a woodpecker; the
nuts rattled down, down, down inside.

'How shall you ever get them out
again? It is like a money box!' said Goody.

'I shall be much thinner before
springtime, my love,' said Timmy
Tiptoes, peeping into the hole.

They did collect quantities — because
they did not lose them! Squirrels who

bury their nuts in the ground lose more than half, because they cannot remember the place.

The most forgetful squirrel in the wood was called Silvertail. He began to dig, but he could not remember where. And then he dug again and found some

nuts that did not belong to him; and there was a fight. And other squirrels began to dig – the whole wood was in commotion!

Unfortunately, just at this time a flock of little birds flew by, from bush to bush, searching for green caterpillars and spiders. There were several sorts of little birds, twittering different songs.

The first one sang – 'Who's bin digging up *my* nuts? Who's-been-digging-up-*my*-nuts?'

And another sang – 'Little bit a bread and *no* cheese! Little-bit-a-bread-an'-*no*-cheese!'

The squirrels followed and listened. The first little bird flew into the bush where Timmy and Goody Tiptoes were

Beatrix Potter

quietly tying up their bags, and it sang —
'Who's bin digging up *my* nuts? Who's-
been-digging-up-*my* -nuts?'

The Tale of Timmy Tiptoes

Timmy Tiptoes went on with his work without replying; indeed, the little bird did not expect an answer. It was only singing its natural song, and it meant nothing at all.

But when the other squirrels heard that song, they rushed upon Timmy Tiptoes and cuffed and scratched him, and upset his bag of nuts. The innocent little bird which had caused all the mischief, flew away in a fright!

Timmy rolled over and over, and then turned tail and fled towards his nest, followed by a crowd of squirrels shouting, 'Who's been digging up *my* nuts?'

They caught
him and
dragged
him up
the
very
same
tree
where
there
was the
little
round hole,
and they pushed him in.

The hole was much too small for Timmy Tiptoes' figure. They squeezed him dreadfully, it was a wonder they did not break his ribs.

'We will leave him here till he confesses,' said Silvertail Squirrel and he shouted into the hole — 'Who's been digging up *my* nuts?'

Timmy Tiptoes made no reply; he had tumbled down inside the tree, upon half a peck of nuts belonging to himself.

He lay quite stunned and still. Goody Tiptoes picked up the nut bags and went home.

She made
a cup of
tea for
Timmy;
but he
didn't come
and didn't
come.

Goody

Tiptoes
passed a lonely
and unhappy night. Next morning she
ventured back to the nut bushes to look
for him; but the other unkind squirrels
drove her away.

She wandered all over the wood,
calling – 'Timmy Tiptoes! Timmy
Tiptoes! Oh, where is Timmy Tiptoes?'

In the meantime Timmy Tiptoes came to his senses. He found himself tucked up in a little moss bed, very much in the dark, feeling sore; it seemed to be underground. Timmy coughed and groaned, because his ribs hurted him. There was a chirpy noise, and a small striped chipmunk appeared with a night-light, and hoped he felt better?

He was most kind to Timmy Tiptoes; he lent him his nightcap; and the house was full of provisions.

The chipmunk explained that it had rained nuts through the top of the tree. 'Besides, I found a few buried!'

He laughed and chuckled when he heard Timmy's story.

While Timmy was confined to bed,

The Tale of Timmy Tiptoes

he 'ticed him to eat quantities – though Timmy protested, 'But how shall I ever get out through that hole unless I thin myself? My wife will be anxious!'

'Just another nut – or two nuts; let me crack them for you,' said the chipmunk.

Timmy Tiptoes grew fatter and fatter!

Now Goody Tiptoes had set to work again by herself. She did not put any more nuts into the woodpecker's hole, because she had always doubted how they could be got out again. She hid them under a tree root; they rattled down, down, down. Once when Goody emptied an extra big bagful, there was a decided squeak; and next time Goody brought another bagful, a little striped chipmunk

scrambled out in a hurry.

'It is getting perfectly full-up downstairs; the sitting-room is full, and they are rolling along the passage; and my husband, Chippy Hackee, has run away and left me. What is the explanation of these showers of nuts?'

'I am sure I beg your pardon; I did not know that anybody lived here,' said Mrs Goody Tiptoes; 'but where is Chippy Hackee? My husband, Timmy Tiptoes, has run away too.'

'I know where Chippy is; a little bird told me,' said Mrs Chippy Hackee.

She led the way to the woodpecker's tree, and they listened at the hole.

Down below there was a noise of nut-crackers, and a fat squirrel voice and a thin squirrel voice were singing together:

> *My little old man and I fell out,*
> *How shall we bring this matter about?*
> *Bring it about as well as you can,*
> *And get you gone, you little old man!'*

'You could squeeze in through that little round hole,' said Goody Tiptoes.

'Yes, I could,' said the chipmunk, 'but my husband, Chippy Hackee, bites!'

Down below there was a noise of cracking nuts and nibbling; and then the

The Tale of Timmy Tiptoes

fat squirrel voice and the thin squirrel voice sang —

'For the diddlum day,
Day diddle dum di!
Day diddle diddle dum day!'

Then Goody peeped in at the hole, and called down – 'Timmy Tiptoes! Oh fie, Timmy Tiptoes, come out at once!'

And Timmy replied, 'Is that you, Goody Tiptoes? Why, certainly!'

He came up and kissed Goody through the hole; but he was so fat that he could not get out.

The Tale of Timmy Tiptoes

Chippy Hackee was not too fat, but he did not want to come out; he stayed down below and chuckled.

And so it went on for a fortnight; till a big wind blew off the top of the tree, and opened up the hole and let in the rain.

Then Timmy Tiptoes came out, and went home with an umbrella.

But Chippy Hackee continued to camp out for another week, although it was uncomfortable.

The Tale of Timmy Tiptoes

At last a large bear came walking through the wood. Perhaps he also was looking for nuts; he seemed to be sniffing around.

Chippy Hackee went home in a hurry!

And when Chippy Hackee got home, he found he had caught a cold in his head; and he was more uncomfortable still.

The Tale of Timmy Tiptoes

And now Timmy and Goody Tiptoes keep their nut-store fastened up with a little padlock.

And whenever that little bird sees the chipmunks, he sings – 'Who's been digging up *my* nuts? Who's-been-digging-up-*my*-nuts?' But nobody ever answers!

The Tale of
Mr Tod

For Francis William of Ulva —
Someday!

I have made many books about well-behaved people. Now, for a change, I am going to make a story about two disagreeable people, called Tommy Brock and Mr Tod.

Nobody could call Mr Tod 'nice'. The rabbits could not bear him; they could smell him half a mile off. He was of a wandering habit and he had foxy whiskers; they never knew where he would be next.

One day he was living in a stick-house

in the coppice, causing terror to the family of old Mr Benjamin Bouncer. Next day he moved into a pollard willow near the lake, frightening the wild ducks and the water rats.

In winter and early spring he might generally be found in an earth among the rocks at the top of Bull Banks, under Oatmeal Crag.

He had half a dozen houses, but he was seldom at home.

The houses were not always empty

when Mr Tod moved *out* because sometimes Tommy Brock moved *in* (without asking leave).

Tommy Brock was a short bristly fat waddling person with a grin; he grinned all over his face. He was not nice in his habits. He ate wasp nests and frogs and worms; and he waddled about by moonlight, digging things up.

His clothes were very dirty; and as he slept in the daytime, he always went to bed in his boots. And the bed which he went to bed in was generally Mr Tod's.

Now Tommy Brock did occasionally eat rabbit pie; but it was only very little young ones occasionally, when other food was really scarce. He was friendly with old Mr Bouncer; they agreed in disliking the wicked otters and Mr Tod; they often talked over that painful subject.

The Tale of Mr Tod

Old Mr Bouncer was stricken in years. He sat in the spring sunshine outside the burrow, in a muffler, smoking a pipe of rabbit tobacco.

He lived with his son Benjamin Bunny and his daughter-in-law Flopsy, who had a young family. Old Mr Bouncer was in charge of the family that afternoon, because Benjamin and Flopsy had gone out.

The little rabbit babies were just old enough to open their blue eyes and kick.

They lay in a fluffy bed of rabbit wool and hay, in a shallow burrow, separate from the main rabbit hole. To tell the truth – old Mr Bouncer had forgotten them.

He sat in the sun, and conversed cordially with Tommy Brock, who was passing through the wood with a sack and a little spud, which he used for digging, and some mole traps. He complained bitterly about the scarcity of pheasants' eggs, and accused Mr Tod

of poaching them. And the otters had cleared off all the frogs while he was asleep in winter – 'I have not had a good square meal for a fortnight. I am living on pig-nuts. I shall have to turn vegetarian and eat my own tail!' said Tommy Brock.

It was not much of a joke, but it tickled old Mr Bouncer, because Tommy Brock was so fat and stumpy and grinning.

So old Mr Bouncer laughed and pressed Tommy Brock to come inside, to taste a slice of seed cake and 'a glass of my daughter Flopsy's cowslip wine'. Tommy Brock squeezed himself into the rabbit hole with alacrity.

Then old Mr Bouncer smoked another pipe, and gave Tommy Brock a cabbage-leaf cigar which was so very strong that it made Tommy Brock grin more than ever; and the smoke filled the burrow. Old Mr Bouncer coughed and laughed; and Tommy Brock puffed and grinned.

And Mr Bouncer laughed and coughed, and shut his eyes because of the cabbage smoke . . .

When Flopsy and Benjamin came back old Mr Bouncer woke up. Tommy Brock and all the young rabbit babies had disappeared!

Mr Bouncer would not confess that he had admitted anybody into the rabbit hole. But the smell of badger was

undeniable; and there were round heavy footmarks in the sand. He was in disgrace; Flopsy wrung her ears, and slapped him.

Benjamin Bunny set off at once after Tommy Brock.

There was not much difficulty in tracking him; he had left his footmarks and gone slowly up the winding footpath through the wood. Here he had rooted up the moss and wood sorrel. There he had dug quite a deep hole for dog darnel and had set a mole trap. A little stream crossed the way. Benjamin skipped lightly over dry-foot; the badger's heavy steps showed plainly in the mud.

The path led to a part of the thicket where the trees had been cleared; there were leafy oak stumps, and a sea of blue hyacinths – but the smell that made Benjamin stop was *not* the smell of flowers!

Mr Tod's stick-house was before him; and, for once, Mr Tod was at home. There was not only a foxy flavour in proof of it – there was smoke coming out of the broken pail that served as a chimney.

Benjamin Bunny sat up, staring; his whiskers twitched. Inside the stick-house somebody dropped a plate and said something. Benjamin stamped his foot, and bolted.

He never stopped till he came to the

other side of the wood. Apparently Tommy Brock had turned the same way. Upon the top of the wall there were again the marks of badger; and some ravellings of a sack had caught on a briar.

Benjamin climbed over the wall, into a meadow. He found another mole trap newly set; he was still upon the track of

Tommy Brock. It was getting late in the afternoon. Other rabbits were coming out to enjoy the evening air. One of them in a blue coat, by himself, was busily hunting for dandelions. 'Cousin Peter! Peter Rabbit, Peter Rabbit!' shouted Benjamin Bunny.

The blue coated rabbit sat up with

pricked ears – 'Whatever is the matter, Cousin Benjamin? Is it a cat? or John Stoat Ferret?'

'No, no, no! He's bagged my family – Tommy Brock – in a sack – have you seen him?'

'Tommy Brock? how many, Cousin Benjamin?'

'Seven, Cousin Peter, and all of them twins! Did he come this way? Please tell me quick!'

'Yes, yes; not ten minutes since . . . He had a sack with something 'live in it; he said they were *caterpillars*; I did think they were kicking rather hard, for caterpillars.'

'Which way? which way has he gone, Cousin Peter?'

'I watched him set a mole trap. Let me

use my mind, Cousin Benjamin; tell me from the beginning.'

Benjamin did so.

'My Uncle Bouncer has displayed a lamentable want of discretion for his years,' said Peter reflectively; 'but there are two hopeful circumstances. Your family is alive and kicking; and Tommy Brock has had refreshments. He will probably go to sleep, and keep them for breakfast.'

'Which way?'

'Cousin Benjamin, compose yourself. I know very well which way. Because Mr Tod was at home in the stick-house, he has gone to Mr Tod's other house, at the top of Bull Banks. I partly know, because he offered to leave any message at Sister Cottontail's; he said he would be passing.'

(Cottontail had married a black rabbit,
and gone to live on the hill.)

Peter hid his dandelions, and
accompanied the afflicted parent, who

was all of a-twitter. They crossed several fields and began to climb the hill; the tracks of Tommy Brock were plainly to be seen. He seemed to have put down the sack every dozen yards to rest.

'He must be very puffed; we are close behind him, by the scent. What a nasty person!' said Peter.

The sunshine was still warm and slanting on the hill pastures. Halfway up, Cottontail was sitting in her doorway, with four or five half-grown little rabbits playing about her, one black and the others brown.

Cottontail had seen Tommy Brock passing in the distance. Asked whether her husband was at home she replied that Tommy Brock had rested twice while she watched him.

He had nodded, and pointed to the sack, and seemed doubled up with laughing.

'Come away, Peter; he will be cooking them; come quicker!' said Benjamin Bunny.

They climbed up and up.

'Cottontail's husband was at home; I saw his black ears peeping out of the hole.'

'They live too near the rocks to quarrel with their neighbours. Come on, Cousin Benjamin!'

When they came near the wood at the top of Bull Banks, they went cautiously. The trees grew among heaped-up rocks; and there, beneath a crag, Mr Tod had made one of his homes. It was at the top

of a steep bank; the rocks and bushes overhung it. The rabbits crept up carefully, listening and peeping.

This house was something between a

cave, a prison and a tumbledown pigsty. There was a strong door, which was shut and locked.

The setting sun made the window panes glow like red flame; but the kitchen fire was not alight. It was neatly laid with dry sticks, as the rabbits could see, when they peeped through the window.

Benjamin sighed with relief.

But there were preparations upon the

kitchen table which made him shudder. There was an immense empty pie dish of blue willow pattern, and a large carving knife and fork, and a chopper.

At the other end of the table was a partly unfolded tablecloth, a plate, a tumbler, a knife and fork, salt cellar, mustard and a chair — in short, preparations for one person's supper.

No person was to be seen, and no young rabbits. The kitchen was empty and silent; the clock had run down. Peter and Benjamin flattened their noses against the window, and stared into the dusk.

Then they scrambled round the rocks to the other side of the house. It was damp and smelly, and overgrown with thorns and briars.

The rabbits shivered in their shoes.

'Oh, my poor rabbit babies! What a dreadful place; I shall never see them again!' sighed Benjamin.

They crept up to the bedroom window. It was closed and bolted like the kitchen's. But there were signs that this window had been recently open; the cobwebs

were disturbed and there were fresh dirty footmarks upon the windowsill.

The room inside was so dark that at first they could make out nothing; but they could hear a noise — a slow deep regular snoring grunt. And as their eyes became accustomed to the darkness, they perceived that somebody was asleep on Mr Tod's bed, curled up under the blanket. 'He has gone to bed in his boots,' whispered Peter.

Benjamin, who was all of a-twitter, pulled Peter off the windowsill.

Tommy Brock's snores continued, grunty and regular, from Mr Tod's bed. Nothing could be seen of the young family.

The sun had set; an owl began to hoot in the wood. There were many unpleasant things lying about that had much better have been buried: rabbit bones and skulls and chickens' legs and other horrors. It was a shocking place, and very dark.

They went back to the front of the house, and tried in every way to move the bolt of the kitchen window. They tried to push up a rusty nail between the window sashes; but it was of no use, especially without a light.

They sat side by side outside the window, whispering and listening.

In half an hour the moon rose over the wood. It shone full and clear and cold upon the house, among the rocks and in at the kitchen window. But alas, no little rabbit babies were to be seen! The moonbeams twinkled on the carving knife and the pie dish, and made a path of brightness across the dirty floor.

The light showed a little door in a wall beside the kitchen fireplace – a little iron door belonging to a brick oven of that old-fashioned sort that used to be heated with faggots of wood.

And presently, at the same moment, Peter and Benjamin noticed that whenever they shook the window the little door opposite shook in answer. The young family was alive and shut up in the oven!

Benjamin was so excited that it was a mercy he did not wake Tommy Brock, whose snores continued solemnly in Mr Tod's bed.

But there really was not very much comfort in the discovery. They could not open the window; and although the young family was alive, the little rabbits were quite incapable of letting themselves out; they were not old enough to crawl.

After much whispering, Peter and Benjamin decided to dig a tunnel. They began to burrow a yard or two lower down the bank. They hoped that they might be able to work between the large stones under the house; the kitchen floor was so dirty that it was impossible to say whether it was made of earth or flags.

They dug and dug for hours. They could not tunnel straight on account of stones; but by the end of the night they were under the kitchen floor. Benjamin was on his back scratching upwards. Peter's claws were worn down; he was outside the tunnel, shuffling sand away. He called out that it was morning — sunrise; and that the jays were making a noise down below in the woods.

Benjamin Bunny came out of the dark tunnel shaking the sand from his ears; he cleaned his face with his paws. Every minute the sun shone warmer on the top of the hill. In the valley there was a sea of white mist, with golden tops of trees showing through.

Again from the fields down below in

the mist there came the angry cry of a jay, followed by the sharp yelping bark of a fox!

Then those two rabbits lost their heads completely. They did the most foolish thing that they could have done. They rushed into their short new tunnel, and hid themselves at the top end of it, under Mr Tod's kitchen floor.

The Tale of Mr Tod

Mr Tod was coming up Bull Banks, and he was in the very worst of tempers. First he had been upset by breaking the plate. It was his own fault; but it was a china plate, the last of the dinner service that had belonged to his grandmother, old Vixen Tod. Then the midges had been very bad. And he had failed to catch a hen pheasant on her nest; and it had contained only five eggs, two of them addled. Mr Tod had had an unsatisfactory night.

As usual, when out of humour, he determined to move house. First he tried the pollard willow, but it was damp; and the otters had left a dead fish near it. Mr Tod likes nobody's leavings but his own.

He made his way up the hill; his temper was not improved by noticing unmistakable marks of badger. No one else grubs up the moss so wantonly as Tommy Brock.

Mr Tod slapped his stick upon the earth and fumed; he guessed where Tommy Brock had gone to. He was further annoyed by the jay bird which followed him persistently. It flew from tree to tree and scolded, warning every rabbit within hearing that either a cat or a fox was coming up the plantation.

The Tale of Mr Tod

Once when it flew screaming over his head Mr Tod snapped at it, and barked.

He approached his house very carefully,

with a large rusty key. He sniffed and his whiskers bristled.

The house was locked up, but Mr Tod had his doubts whether it was empty. He turned the rusty key in the lock; the rabbits below could hear it. Mr Tod opened the door cautiously and went in.

The sight that met Mr Tod's eyes in Mr Tod's kitchen made Mr Tod furious.

There was Mr Tod's chair, and Mr Tod's pie dish, and his knife and fork and mustard and salt cellar, and his tablecloth, that he had left folded up in the dresser — all set out for supper (or breakfast) — without doubt for that odious Tommy Brock.

There was a smell of fresh earth and dirty badger, which fortunately overpowered all smell of rabbit.

But what absorbed Mr Tod's attention was a noise, a deep slow regular snoring, grunting noise, coming from his own bed.

He peeped through the hinges of the half-open bedroom door. Then he turned and came out of the house in a hurry. His whiskers bristled and his coat-collar stood on end with rage.

For the next twenty minutes Mr Tod kept creeping cautiously into the house, and retreating hurriedly out again. By degrees he ventured farther in — right into the bedroom. When he was outside the house, he scratched up the earth with fury. But when he was inside — he did not like the look of Tommy Brock's teeth.

He was lying on his back with his mouth open, grinning from ear to ear. He snored peacefully and regularly; but one eye was not perfectly shut.

Mr Tod came in and out of the bedroom. Twice he brought in his walking stick, and once he brought in the coal scuttle. But he thought better of it, and took them away.

When he came back after removing the coal scuttle, Tommy Brock was lying a little more sideways; but he seemed even sounder asleep. He was an incurably indolent person; he was not in the least afraid of Mr Tod; he was simply too lazy and comfortable to move.

Mr Tod came back yet again into the

bedroom with a clothes-line. He stood a minute watching Tommy Brock and listening attentively to the snores. They were very loud indeed, but seemed quite natural.

Mr Tod turned his back towards the bed, and undid the window. It creaked; he turned round with a jump. Tommy Brock, who had opened one eye – shut it hastily. The snores continued.

Mr Tod's proceedings were peculiar, and rather difficult (because the bed was between the window and the door of

the bedroom). He opened the window a little way, and pushed out the greater part of the clothes-line on to the window-sill. The rest of the line, with a hook at the end, remained in his hand.

Tommy Brock snored conscientiously. Mr Tod stood and looked at him for a minute; then he left the room again.

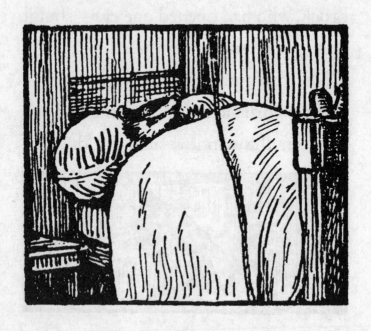

Tommy Brock opened both eyes, and looked at the rope and grinned. There was a noise outside the window. Tommy Brock shut his eyes in a hurry.

Mr Tod had gone out at the front door, and round to the back of the house. On the way, he stumbled over the rabbit burrow. If he had had any idea who was inside it he would have pulled them out quickly.

His foot went through the tunnel nearly upon the top of Peter Rabbit and Benjamin; but, fortunately, he thought that it was some more of Tommy Brock's work.

He took up the coil of line from the sill, listened for a moment, and then tied the rope to a tree.

Tommy Brock watched him with one eye, through the window. He was puzzled.

Mr Tod fetched a large heavy pailful of water from the spring and staggered with it through the kitchen into his bed-room.

Tommy Brock snored industriously, with rather a snort.

Mr Tod put down the pail beside the

bed, took up the end of rope with the hook – hesitated, and looked at Tommy Brock. The snores were almost apoplectic; but the grin was not quite so big.

Mr Tod gingerly mounted a chair by the head of the bedstead. His legs were dangerously near to Tommy Brock's teeth.

He reached up and put the end of rope, with the hook, over the head of the tester bed, where the curtains ought to hang.

(Mr Tod's curtains were folded up and put away, owing to the house being unoccupied. So was the counterpane. Tommy Brock was covered with a blanket only.) Mr Tod standing on the unsteady chair looked down upon him attentively; he really was a first-prize sound sleeper!

It seemed as though nothing would wake him – not even the flapping rope across the bed.

Mr Tod descended safely from the chair, and endeavoured to get up again with the pail of water. He intended to

The Tale of Mr Tod

hang it from the hook, dangling over the
head of Tommy Brock, in order to make
a sort of shower-bath, worked by a string
through the window.

But, naturally, being a thin-legged person (though vindictive and sandy whiskered) – he was quite unable to lift the heavy weight to the level of the hook and rope. He very nearly overbalanced himself.

The snores became more and more apoplectic. One of Tommy Brock's hind

legs twitched under the blanket, but still he slept on peacefully.

Mr Tod and the pail descended from the chair without accident. After considerable thought, he emptied the water into a wash basin and jug. The empty pail was not too heavy for him; he slung it up, wobbling, over the head of Tommy Brock.

Surely there never was such a sleeper! Mr Tod got up and down, down and up on the chair.

As he could not lift the whole pailful of water at once he fetched a milk jug and ladled quarts of water into the pail by degrees. The pail got fuller and fuller, and swung like a pendulum. Occasionally a drop splashed over; but still Tommy

Brock snored regularly and never moved — except for one eye.

At last Mr Tod's preparations were complete. The pail was full of water; the rope was tightly strained over the top of the bed, and across the windowsill to the tree outside.

'It will make a great mess in my bedroom; but I could never sleep in that bed

again without a spring cleaning of some sort,' said Mr Tod.

Mr Tod took a last look at the badger and softly left the room. He went out of the house, shutting the front door. The rabbits heard his footsteps over the tunnel.

He ran round behind the house, intending to undo the rope in order to let fall the pailful of water upon Tommy Brock —

'I will wake him up with an unpleasant surprise,' said Mr Tod.

The moment he had gone, Tommy Brock got up in a hurry; he rolled Mr Tod's dressing-gown into a bundle, put it into the bed beneath the pail of water instead of himself, and left the room also — grinning immensely.

He went into the kitchen, lighted the fire and boiled the kettle; for the moment he did not trouble himself to cook the baby rabbits.

When Mr Tod got to the tree, he found that the weight and strain had dragged the knot so tight that it was past untying. He was obliged to gnaw it with his teeth. He chewed and gnawed for more than twenty minutes. At last the rope gave way with such a sudden jerk that it nearly pulled his teeth out, and quite knocked him over backwards.

Inside the house there was a great crash and splash, and the noise of a pail rolling over and over.

But no screams. Mr Tod was mystified;

he sat quite still, and listened attentively. Then he peeped in at the window. The water was dripping from the bed, the pail had rolled into a corner.

In the middle of the bed, under the blanket, was a wet flattened *something* — much flattened in the middle, where the pail had caught it (as it were across the tummy). Its head was covered by the wet blanket, and it was *not snoring any longer*.

There was nothing stirring, and no sound except the drip, drop, drop, drip of water trickling from the mattress.

Mr Tod watched it for half an hour; his eyes glistened.

Then he cut a caper, and became so bold that he even tapped at the window; but the bundle never moved.

Yes — there was no doubt about it — it had turned out even better than he had planned; the pail had hit poor old Tommy Brock, and killed him dead!

'I will bury that nasty person in the hole which he has dug. I will bring my bedding out, and dry it in the sun,' said Mr Tod.

'I will wash the tablecloth and spread it on the grass in the sun to bleach. And the blanket must be hung up in the wind; and the bed must be thoroughly dis-infected and aired with a warming-pan and warmed with a hot-water bottle.

'I will get soft soap, and monkey soap, and all sorts of soap; and soda and scrubbing brushes; and Persian powder; and carbolic to remove the smell. I must

have a disinfecting. Perhaps I may have to burn sulphur.'

He hurried round the house to get a shovel from the kitchen – 'First I will arrange the hole – then I will drag out that person in the blanket . . .'

He opened the door . . .

Tommy Brock was sitting at Mr Tod's kitchen table, pouring out tea from Mr Tod's teapot into Mr Tod's teacup. He was quite dry himself and grinning, and he threw the cup of scalding tea all over Mr Tod.

Then Mr Tod rushed upon Tommy Brock and Tommy Brock grappled with Mr Tod among the broken crockery, and there was a terrific battle all over the kitchen. To the rabbits underneath it

sounded as if the floor would give way at each crash of falling furniture.

They crept out of their tunnel and hung about among the rocks and bushes, listening anxiously.

Inside the house the racket was fearful. The rabbit babies in the oven woke up trembling; perhaps it was fortunate they were shut up inside.

Everything was upset except the kitchen table. And everything was broken, except the mantelpiece and the kitchen fender. The crockery was smashed to atoms.

The chairs were broken, and the window, and the clock fell with a crash, and there were handfuls of Mr Tod's sandy whiskers.

The vases fell off the mantelpiece, the cannisters fell off the shelf; the kettle fell off the hob. Tommy Brock put his foot in a jar of raspberry jam.

And the boiling water out of the kettle fell upon the tail of Mr Tod.

When the kettle fell, Tommy Brock, who was still grinning, happened to be uppermost, and he rolled Mr Tod over and over like a log, out of the door.

Then the snarling and worrying went on outside; and they rolled over the bank and downhill, bumping over the rocks.

As soon as the coast was clear, Peter Rabbit and Benjamin Bunny came out of the bushes.

'Now for it! Run in, Cousin Benjamin! Run in and get them! while I watch the door.'

But Benjamin was frightened – 'Oh! oh! they are coming back!'

'No, they are not.'

'Yes, they are!'

'What dreadful bad language! I think they have fallen down the stone quarry.'

Still Benjamin hesitated, and Peter kept pushing him – 'Be quick, it's all right. Shut the oven door, Cousin Benjamin, so that he won't miss them.'

Decidedly there were lively doings in
Mr Tod's kitchen!

At home in the rabbit hole, things had
not been quite comfortable.

After quarrelling at supper, Flopsy and
old Mr Bouncer had passed a sleepless
night, and quarrelled again at breakfast.

Old Mr Bouncer could no longer deny that he had invited company into the rabbit hole; but he refused to reply to the questions and reproaches of Flopsy. The day passed heavily.

Old Mr Bouncer, very sulky, was huddled up in a corner, barricaded with a chair. Flopsy had taken away his pipe

and hidden the tobacco. She had been having a complete turn-out and spring clean, to relieve her feelings. She had just finished. Old Mr Bouncer, behind his chair, was wondering anxiously what she would do next.

In Mr Tod's kitchen, amid the wreckage, Benjamin Bunny picked his way to the oven nervously, through a thick cloud of dust. He opened the oven door, felt inside, and found something warm and wriggling. He lifted it out carefully, and rejoined Peter Rabbit.

'I've got them! Can we get away? Shall we hide, Cousin Peter?'

Peter pricked his ears; distant sounds of fighting still echoed in the wood.

Five minutes afterwards two breathless

rabbits came scuttering away down Bull
Banks, half carrying, half dragging a sack
between them, bumpetty-bump over the
grass. They reached home safely, and
burst into the rabbit hole.

Great was old Mr Bouncer's relief and Flopsy's joy when Peter and Benjamin arrived in triumph with the young family. The rabbit babies were rather tumbled and very hungry; they were fed and put to bed. They soon recovered.

A new long pipe and a fresh supply of rabbit tobacco was presented to Mr

Bouncer. He was rather upon his dignity; but he accepted.

Old Mr Bouncer was forgiven, and they all had dinner. Then Peter and Benjamin told their story — but they had not waited long enough to be able to tell the end of the battle between Tommy Brock and Mr Tod.

* * *

There will never be any love lost between Tommy Brock and Mr Tod.

The Tale of Johnny Town-Mouse

To Aesop in the shadows

Johnny Town-Mouse was born in a cupboard. Timmy Willie was born in a
garden. Timmy Willie was a little country
mouse who went to town by mistake in a
hamper. The gardener sent vegetables to
town once a week by carrier; he packed
them in a big hamper.

The gardener left the hamper by the garden gate, so that the carrier could pick it up when he passed. Timmy Willie crept in through a hole in the wickerwork – and after eating some peas, Timmy Willie fell fast asleep.

He awoke in a fright, while the hamper was being lifted into the carrier's cart. Then there was a jolting, and the

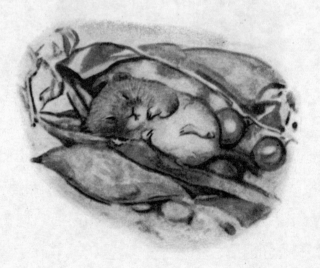

clattering of a horse's feet; other packages were thrown in; for miles and miles – jolt – jolt – jolt! and Timmy Willie trembled among the jumbled-up vegetables.

At last the cart stopped at a house, where the hamper was taken out, carried in and set down. The cook gave the carrier sixpence; the back door banged, and the cart rumbled away. But there was no quiet; there seemed to be

hundreds of carts passing. Dogs barked; boys whistled in the street; the cook laughed, the parlour maid ran upstairs and downstairs; and a canary sang like a steam engine.

Timmy Willie, who had lived all his life in a garden, was almost frightened to death. Presently the cook opened the hamper and began to unpack the vegetables. Out sprang the terrified Timmy Willie.

Up jumped the cook on a chair, exclaiming, 'A mouse! a mouse! Call the cat! Fetch me the poker, Sarah!' Timmy Willie did not wait for Sarah with the poker; he rushed along the skirting board till he came to a little hole, and in he popped.

He dropped half a foot, and crashed into the middle of a mouse-dinner party, breaking three glasses. 'Who in the world is this?' enquired Johnny Town-Mouse. But after the first exclamation of surprise he instantly recovered his manners.

With the utmost politeness he introduced Timmy Willie to nine other mice, all with long tails and white neckties. Timmy Willie's own tail was insignificant. Johnny Town-Mouse and his

friends noticed it; but they were too well bred to make personal remarks; only one of them asked Timmy Willie if he had ever been in a trap?

The dinner was of eight courses; not much of anything, but truly elegant. All the dishes were unknown to Timmy Willie, who would have been a little

afraid of tasting them, only he was very hungry and very anxious to behave with company manners. The continual noise upstairs made him so nervous that he dropped a plate.

'Never mind, they don't belong to us,' said Johnny. 'Why don't those youngsters come back with the dessert?'

It should be explained that two young

mice, who were waiting on the others, went skirmishing upstairs to the kitchen between courses. Several times they had come tumbling in, squeaking and laughing; Timmy Willie learnt with horror that they were being chased by the cat. His appetite failed, he felt faint.

'Try some jelly?' said Johnny Town-

Mouse. 'No? Would you rather go to bed? I will show you a most comfortable sofa pillow.'

The sofa pillow had a hole in it. Johnny Town-Mouse quite honestly recommended it as the best bed, kept exclusively for visitors. But the sofa smelt of cat. Timmy Willie preferred to spend a miserable night under the fender.

It was just the same next day. An excellent breakfast was provided – for mice accustomed to eat bacon; but Timmy Willie had been reared on roots and salad. Johnny Town-Mouse and his friends racketted about under the floors and came boldly

out all over the house in the evening.

One particularly loud crash had been caused by Sarah tumbling downstairs

with the tea-tray; there were crumbs and sugar and smears of jam to be collected, in spite of the cat.

Timmy Willie longed to be at home in his peaceful nest in a sunny bank. The food disagreed with him; the noise prevented him from sleeping. In a few days he grew so thin that Johnny Town-Mouse noticed it, and questioned him. He listened to Timmy Willie's story and enquired about the garden. 'It sounds rather a dull place? What do you do when it rains?'

'When it rains, I sit in my little sandy burrow and shell corn and seeds from my autumn store. I peep out at the throstles and blackbirds on the lawn, and my friend Cock Robin. And when

the sun comes out again, you should see my garden and the flowers – roses and pinks and pansies – no noise except the birds and bees, and the lambs in the meadows.'

'There goes that cat again!' exclaimed Johnny Town-Mouse. When they had taken refuge in the coal-cellar he resumed the conversation: 'I confess I am a little disappointed; we have endeavoured to entertain you, Timothy William.'

'Oh yes, yes, you have been most kind; but I do feel so ill,' said Timmy Willie.

'It may be that your teeth and digestion are unaccustomed to our food; perhaps it might be wiser for you to return in the hamper.'

'Oh? Oh!' cried Timmy Willie.

'Why, of course, for the matter of that we could have sent you back last week,' said Johnny rather huffily; 'did you not know that the hamper goes back empty on Saturdays?'

The Tale of Johnny Town-Mouse

So Timmy Willie said goodbye to his new friends, and hid in the hamper with a crumb of cake and a withered cabbage leaf; and after much jolting, he was set down safely in his own garden.

Sometimes on Saturdays he went to look at the hamper lying by the gate, but he knew better than to get in again. And nobody got out, though Johnny Town-Mouse had half promised a visit.

The winter passed; the sun came out again; Timmy Willie sat by his burrow

The Tale of Johnny Town-Mouse

warming his little fur coat and sniffing the smell of violets and spring grass. He had nearly forgotten his visit to town when up the sandy path, all spick and span with a brown leather bag, came Johnny Town-Mouse!

Timmy Willie received him with open arms. 'You have come at the best of all

the year; we will have herb pudding and sit in the sun.'

'Hmm! it is a little damp,' said Johnny Town-Mouse, who was carrying his tail under his arm, out of the mud.

'What is that fearful noise?' he started violently.

'That?' said Timmy Willie, 'that is only a cow; I will beg a little milk; they are quite harmless, unless they happen to lie down upon you. How are all our friends?'

Johnny's account was rather middling. He explained why he was paying his visit

so early in the season; the family had gone to the seaside for Easter; the cook was doing spring cleaning, on board wages, with particular instructions to clear out the mice. There were four kittens, and the cat had killed the canary.

'They say we did it; but I know better,' said Johnny Town-Mouse. 'Whatever is that fearful racket?'

'That is only the lawn-mower; I will fetch some of the grass clippings presently

to make your bed. I am sure you had better settle in the country, Johnny.'

'H'mm – we shall see by Tuesday week; the hamper is stopped while they are at the seaside.'

'I am sure you will never want to live in town again,' said Timmy Willie.

But he did. He went back in the very next hamper of vegetables; he said it was too quiet!!

One place suits one person, another place suits another person. For my part

I prefer to live in the country, like
Timmy Willie.

The Tale of Little
Pig Robinson

Chapter I

When I was a child, I used to go to the seaside for the holidays. We stayed in a little town where there was a harbour and fishing boats and fishermen. They sailed away to catch herrings in nets. When the boats came back home again some had only caught a few herrings. Others had caught so many that they could not all be unloaded on to the quay. Then horses and carts were driven into the shallow water at low tide to meet the heavily laden boats. The fish were shovelled over the side of the boat into the carts and taken to the railway station, where a special train of fish trucks was waiting.

Great was the excitement when the fishing boats returned with a good catch of herrings. Half the people in the town ran down to the quay, including cats.

There was a white cat called Susan who never missed meeting the boats. She belonged to the wife of an old fisherman named Sam. The wife's name was Betsy. She had rheumatics, and she had no family except Susan and five hens. Betsy sat by the fire; her back ached; she said, 'Ow! Ow!' whenever she had to put coal on, and stir the pot. Susan sat opposite to Betsy. She felt sorry for Betsy; she wished she knew how to put the coal on and stir the pot. All day long they sat by

the fire while Sam was away fishing.
They had a cup of tea and some milk.

'Susan,' said Betsy, 'I can hardly stand
up. Go to the front gate and look out for
master's boat.'

Susan went out and came back. Three
or four times she went out into the
garden. At last, late in the afternoon, she
saw the sails of the fishing fleet, coming
in over the sea.

'Go down to the harbour; ask master for six herrings; I will cook them for supper. Take my basket, Susan.'

Susan took the basket; also she borrowed Betsy's bonnet and little plaid shawl. I saw her hurrying down to the harbour.

Other cats were coming out of the cottages, and running down the steep streets that lead to the seafront. Also ducks. I remember that they were most peculiar ducks with top-knots that looked like tam-o'-shanter caps. Everybody was hurrying to meet the boats – nearly everybody. I only met one person, a dog called Stumpy, who was going the opposite way. He was carrying a paper parcel in his mouth.

Some dogs do not care for fish. Stumpy had been to the butcher's to buy mutton chops for himself and Bob and Percy and Miss Rose. Stumpy was a large, serious, well-behaved brown dog with a short tail. He lived with Bob the retriever and Percy the cat and Miss Rose who kept house. Stumpy had belonged to a very rich old gentleman and when the old gentleman died he left money to Stumpy – ten shillings a week for the rest of Stumpy's life. So that was why Stumpy and Bob and Percy the cat all lived together in a pretty little house.

Susan with her basket met Stumpy at the corner of Broad Street. Susan made a curtsy. She would have stopped to enquire after Percy, only she was in a hurry to meet the boat. Percy was lame; he had hurt his foot. It had been trapped under the wheel of a milk cart.

Stumpy looked at Susan out of the

corner of his eye; he wagged his tail, but he did not stop. He could not bow or say 'Good-afternoon' for fear of dropping the parcel of mutton chops. He turned out of Broad Street into Woodbine Lane, where he lived; he pushed open the front door and disappeared into the house. Presently there was a smell of cooking, and I have no doubt that Stumpy and Bob and Miss Rose enjoyed their mutton chops.

Percy could not be found at dinner time. He had slipped out of the window and, like all the other cats in the town, he had gone to meet the fishing boats.

Susan hurried along Broad Street and took the short cut to the harbour, down a steep flight of steps. The ducks had wisely gone another way, round by the seafront. The steps were too steep and slippery for anyone less sure-footed than a cat. Susan went down quickly and easily. There were forty-three steps, rather dark and slimy, between high backs of houses.

A smell of ropes and pitch and a good deal of noise came up from below. At the bottom of the steps was the quay, or landing-place, beside the inner harbour.

The tide was out; there was no water; the vessels rested on the dirty mud. Several ships were moored beside the quay; others were anchored inside the breakwater.

Near the steps, coal was being unloaded from two grimy colliers called the *Margery Dawe* of Sunderland and the

Jenny Jones of Cardiff. Men ran along planks with wheelbarrows full of coal; coal scoops were swung ashore by cranes, and emptied with a loud thumping and rattling.

Farther along the quay, another ship called the *Pound of Candles* was taking a mixed cargo on board. Bales, casks, packing-cases, barrels — all manner of goods were being stowed into the hold; sailors and stevedores shouted; chains rattled and clanked. Susan waited for an opportunity to slip past the noisy crowd. She watched a cask of cider that bobbed and swung in the air on its passage from the quay to the deck of the *Pound of Candles*. A yellow cat who sat in the rigging was also watching the cask.

The rope ran through the pulley; the
cask went down bobbitty on to the deck,
where a sailor man was waiting for it.
Said the sailor down below: 'Look out!

Mind your head, young sir! Stand out of the way!'

'Wee, wee, wee!' grunted a small pink pig, scampering round the deck of the *Pound of Candles*.

The yellow cat in the rigging watched the small pink pig. The yellow cat in the rigging looked across at Susan on the quay. The yellow cat winked.

Susan was surprised to see a pig on board a ship. But she was in a hurry. She threaded her way along the quay, among coal and cranes and men wheeling hand-trucks and noises and smells. She passed the fish auction, and fish boxes, and fish sorters, and barrels that women were filling with herrings and salt.

Seagulls swooped and screamed.

Beatrix Potter

Hundreds of fish boxes and tons of fresh fish were being loaded into the hold of a small steamer. Susan was glad to get away from the crowd, down a much shorter flight of steps, on to the shore of the outer harbour. The ducks arrived soon afterwards, waddling and quacking. And old Sam's boat, the *Betsy Timmins*, last of the herring fleet and heavy laden, came in round the breakwater and drove her blunt nose into the shingle.

Sam was in high spirits; he had had a big catch. He and his mate and two lads commenced to unload their fish into carts, as the tide was too low to float the fishing boat up to the quay. The boat was full of herrings.

But, good luck or bad luck, Sam never failed to throw a handful of herrings to Susan.

'Here's for the two old girls and a hot supper! Catch them, Susan! Honest now! There's a broken fish for you! Now take the others to Betsy.'

The ducks were dabbling and gobbling; the seagulls were screaming and swooping. Susan climbed the steps with her basket of herrings and went home by back streets.

Old Betsy cooked two herrings for herself and Susan, another two for Sam's supper when he came in. Then she went to bed with a hot bottle wrapped in a flannel petticoat to help her rheumatics.

Sam ate his supper and smoked a pipe by the fire; and then he went to bed. But Susan sat a long time by the fire, considering. She considered many things — fish, and ducks, and Percy with a lame foot, and dogs that eat mutton chops, and the yellow cat on the ship, and the pig. Susan thought it strange to see a pig upon a ship called the *Pound of Candles*. The mice peeped out from under the cupboard door. The cinders fell together on the hearth. Susan purred gently in her sleep and dreamed of fish and pigs. She could not understand that pig on board a ship. But I know all about him!

Chapter 2

You remember the song about the Owl and the Pussy Cat and their beautiful pea-green boat? How they took some honey and plenty of money, wrapped up in a five-pound note?

They sailed away, for a year and a day,
To the land where the bong tree grows —
And, there in a wood, a piggy-wig stood,
With a ring at the end of his nose — his nose,
With a ring at the end of his nose.

Now I am going to tell you the story of that pig, and why he went to live in the land of the bong tree.

When that pig was little he lived in

Devonshire, with his aunts, Miss Dorcas and Miss Porcas, at a farm called Piggery Porcombe. Their cosy thatched cottage was in an orchard at the top of a steep red Devonshire lane.

The soil was red, the grass was green; and far away below in the distance they could see red cliffs and a bit of bright blue sea. Ships with white sails sailed over the sea into the harbour of Stymouth.

I have often remarked that the Devonshire farms have very strange names. If you had ever seen Piggery Porcombe you would think that the people who lived there were very queer too! Aunt Dorcas was a stout speckled pig who kept hens. Aunt Porcas was a large smiling black pig who took in washing. We shall not hear very much about them in this story. They led prosperous uneventful lives, and their end was bacon. But their nephew Robinson had the most peculiar adventures that ever happened to a pig.

Little pig Robinson was a charming

little fellow; pinky white with small blue eyes, fat cheeks and a double chin, and a turned-up nose with a real silver ring in it. Robinson could see that ring if he shut one eye and squinted sideways.

He was always contented and happy. All day long he ran about the farm, singing little songs to himself, and grunting, 'Wee, wee, wee!' His aunts missed those little songs sadly after Robinson had left them.

'Wee? Wee? Wee?' he answered when anybody spoke to him. 'Wee? Wee? Wee?' listening with his head on one side and one eye screwed up.

Robinson's old aunts fed him and petted him and kept him on the trot.

'Robinson! Robinson!' called Aunt

Dorcas. 'Come quick! I hear a hen clucking. Fetch me the egg; don't break it now!'

'Wee, wee, wee!' answered Robinson, like a little Frenchman.

'Robinson! Robinson! I've dropped a clothes peg, come and pick it up for me!' called Aunt Porcas from the drying green (she being almost too fat to stoop down and pick up anything).

'Wee, wee, wee!' answered Robinson.

Both the aunts were very, very stout. And the stiles in the neighbourhood of Stymouth are narrow.

The footpath from Piggery Porcombe, a red trodden track between short green grass and daisies, crosses many fields. And wherever the footpath crosses over from one field to another field, there is sure to be a stile in the hedge.

'It is not me that is too stout; it is the stiles that are too thin,' said Aunt Dorcas to Aunt Porcas. 'Could you manage to squeeze through them if I stayed at home?'

'I could *not*. Not for two years I could *not*,' replied Aunt Porcas. 'Aggravating, it *is* aggravating of that carrier man to go and upset his donkey cart the day before market day. And eggs at two and tuppence a dozen! How far do you call it to walk all the way round by the road instead of crossing the fields?'

'Four miles if it's one,' sighed Aunt Porcas, 'and me using my last bit of soap. However shall we get our shopping done? The donkey says the cart will take a week to mend.'

'Don't you think you could squeeze through the stiles if you went before dinner?'

'No, I don't, I would stick fast; and so would you,' said Aunt Porcas.

'Don't you think we might venture — ' commenced Aunt Dorcas.

'Venture to send Robinson by the footpath to Stymouth?' finished Aunt Porcas.

'Wee, wee, wee!' answered Robinson.

'I scarcely like to send him alone, though he is sensible for his size.'

'Wee, wee, wee!' answered Robinson.

'But there is nothing else to be done,' said Aunt Dorcas.

So Robinson was popped into the washtub with the last bit of soap. He was scrubbed and dried and polished as bright as a new pin. Then he was dressed in a little blue cotton frock and knickers, and instructed to go shopping to Stymouth with a big market basket.

In the basket were two dozen eggs, a bunch of daffodils, two spring cauliflowers; also Robinson's dinner of bread-and-jam sandwiches. The eggs and flowers and vegetables he must sell in the market, and he must bring back various other purchases from shopping.

'Now take care of yourself in Stymouth, Nephew Robinson. Beware of gunpowder, and ships' cooks, and pantechnicons, and sausages, and shoes, and ships, and sealing-wax. Remember the blue bag, the soap, the darning-wool — what was the other thing?' said Aunt Dorcas.

'The darning-wool, the soap, the blue bag, the yeast — what was the other thing?' said Aunt Porcas.

'Wee, wee, wee!' answered Robinson.

'The blue bag, the soap, the yeast, the darning-wool, the cabbage seed — that's five, and there ought to be six. It was two more than four because it was two too many to tie knots in the corners of his hankie to remember by. Six to buy, it should be — '

'I have it!' said Aunt Porcas. 'It was tea — tea, blue bag, soap, darning-wool, yeast, cabbage seed.

You will buy most of them at Mr Mumby's. Explain about the carrier, Robinson; tell him we will bring the washing and some more vegetables next week.'

'Wee, wee, wee!' answered Robinson, setting off with the big basket.

Aunt Dorcas and Aunt Porcas stood in the porch. They watched him safely out of sight, down the field, and over the first of the many stiles. When they went back to their household tasks they were grunty and snappy with each other, because they were uneasy about Robinson.

'I wish we had not let him go. You and your tiresome blue bag!' said Aunt Dorcas.

'Blue bag, indeed! It was your darning-wool and eggs!' grumbled Aunt Porcas. 'Bother that carrier man and his donkey cart! Why could not he keep out of the ditch until after market day?'

Chapter 3

The walk to Stymouth was a long one, in spite of going by the fields. But the footpath ran downhill all the way, and

Robinson was merry. He sang his little song, for joy of the fine morning, and he chuckled, 'Wee, wee, wee!' Larks were singing, too, high overhead.

And higher still – high up against the blue sky, the great white gulls sailed in wide circles. Their hoarse cries came softened back to earth from a great way up above. Important rooks and lively jackdaws strutted about the meadows among the daisies and buttercups.

Lambs skipped and baa'ed; the sheep looked round at Robinson.

'Mind yourself in Stymouth, little pig,' said a motherly ewe.

Robinson trotted on until he was out of breath and very hot. He had crossed five big fields, and ever so many stiles:

stiles with steps; ladder stiles; stiles of
wooden posts; some of them were very
awkward with a heavy basket. The farm
of Piggery Porcombe was no longer
in sight when he looked back. In the

distance before him, beyond the farm-lands and cliffs – never any nearer – the dark-blue sea rose like a wall.

Robinson sat down to rest beside a hedge in a sheltered sunny spot. Yellow pussy-willow catkins were in flower above his head; there were primroses in hundreds on the bank and a warm smell of moss and grass and steaming moist red earth.

'If I eat my dinner now, I shall not have to carry it. Wee, wee, wee!' said Robinson.

The walk had made him so hungry he would have liked to eat an egg as well as the jam sandwiches; but he had been too well brought up.

'It would spoil the two dozen,' said Robinson.

He picked a bunch of primroses and tied them up with a bit of darning-wool that Aunt Dorcas had given him for a pattern.

'I will sell them in the market for my very own self, and buy sweeties with my pennies. How many pennies have I got?' said Robinson, feeling in his pocket. 'One from Aunt Dorcas, and one from Aunt Porcas, and one for my primroses for my very own self — oh, wee, wee, wee! There is somebody trotting along the road! I shall be late for market!'

Robinson jumped up and pushed his basket through a very narrow stile where the footpath crossed into the public road. He saw a man on horseback. Old Mr Pepperil came up, riding a chestnut horse with white legs. His two tall grey-hounds ran before him; they looked through the bars of the gates into every field that they passed. They came bounding up to Robinson, very large

and friendly; they licked his face and asked what he had got in that basket. Mr Pepperil called them. 'Here, Pirate! Here, Postboy! Come here, sir!' He did not wish to be answerable for the eggs.

The road had been recently covered with sharp new flints. Mr Pepperil walked the chestnut horse on the grass edge, and talked to Robinson. He was a jolly old gentleman, very affable, with a red face and white whiskers. All the green fields and red ploughland between Stymouth and Piggery Porcombe belonged to him.

'Hello, hello! And where are you off to, little pig Robinson?'

'Please, Mr Pepperil, sir, I'm going to market. Wee, wee, wee!' said Robinson.

'What, all by yourself? Where are Miss Dorcas and Miss Porcas? Not ill, I trust?'

Robinson explained about the narrow stiles.

'Dear, dear! Too fat, too fat? So you are going all alone? Why don't your aunts keep a dog to run errands?'

Robinson answered all Mr Pepperil's questions very sensibly and prettily. He showed much intelligence, and quite a good knowledge of vegetables, for one so young. He trotted along almost under the horse, looking up at its shiny chestnut coat, and the broad white girth, and Mr Pepperil's gaiters and brown leather boots. Mr Pepperil was pleased with Robinson; he gave him another penny.

The Tale of Little Pig Robinson

At the end of the flints, he gathered up the reins and touched the horse with his heel.

'Well, good day, little pig. Kind regards to the aunts. Mind yourself in Stymouth.' He whistled for his dogs, and trotted away.

Robinson continued to walk along the road. He passed by an orchard where seven thin dirty pigs were grubbing. They had no silver rings in their noses! He crossed Styford Bridge without stopping to look over the parapet at the little fishes, swimming head upstream, balanced in the sluggish current; or the white ducks that dabbled among floating masses of water-crowsfoot. At Styford Mill he called to leave a message from

Aunt Dorcas to the miller about meal; the miller's wife gave him an apple.

At the house beyond the mill there is a big dog that barks; but the big dog Gypsy only smiled and wagged his tail at Robinson. Several carts and gigs overtook him. First, two old farmers who screwed themselves round to stare at Robinson. They had two geese, a sack of potatoes and some cabbages sitting on the back seat of their gig. Then an old woman passed in a donkey cart with seven hens, and long pink bundles of rhubarb that had been grown in straw under apple barrels. Then with a rattle and a jingle of cans came Robinson's cousin, little Tom Pigg, driving a strawberry-roan pony in a milk float.

He might have offered Robinson a lift, only he happened to be going in the opposite direction; in fact, the strawberry-roan pony was running away home.

'This little pig went to market!' shouted little Tom Pigg gaily, as he rattled out of sight in a cloud of dust, leaving Robinson standing in the road.

Robinson walked on along the road, and presently he came to another stile in the opposite hedge, where the footpath followed the fields again. Robinson got his basket through the stile. For the first time he felt some apprehension. In this field there were cows: big sleek Devon cattle, dark-red like their native soil. The leader of the herd was a vicious old cow, with brass balls screwed on to the tips of her horns. She stared disagreeably at Robinson. He sidled across the meadow and got out through the farther stile as quickly as he could. Here the new-trodden footpath followed round the edge of a crop of young green wheat.

The Tale of Little Pig Robinson

Someone let off a gun with a bang that
made Robinson jump and cracked one
of Aunt Dorcas's eggs in the basket.

A cloud of rooks and jackdaws rose

cawing and scolding from the wheat. Other sounds mingled with their cries; noises of the town of Stymouth that began to come in sight through the elm trees that bordered the fields; distant noises from the station: whistling of an engine, the bump of trucks shunting, noise of workshops; the hum of a distant town; the hooter of a steamer entering the harbour. High overhead came the hoarse cry of the gulls and the squabbling cawing of rooks, old and young, in their rookery up in the elm trees.

Robinson left the fields for the last time and joined a stream of country people on foot and in carts, all going to Stymouth Market.

Chapter 4

Stymouth is a pretty little town, situated at the mouth of the River Pigsty, whose sluggish waters slide gently into a bay sheltered by high red headlands. The town itself seems to be sliding downhill in a basin of hills, all slipping seaward into Stymouth harbour, which is surrounded by quays and the outer breakwater.

The outskirts of the town are untidy, as is frequently the case with seaports. A straggling suburb on the western approach is inhabited principally by goats, and persons who deal in old iron, rags, tarred rope and fishing nets. There are rope walks and washing that flaps on waggling lines above banks of stony shingle, littered with seaweed, whelk shells and dead crabs — very different from Aunt Porcas's clothes-lines over the clean green grass.

And there are marine stores that sell spyglasses, and sou'westers, and onions; and there are smells; and curious high sheds, shaped like sentry boxes, where they hang up herring nets to dry; and loud talking inside dirty houses. It seemed a likely place to meet a pantechnicon. Robinson kept in the middle of the road. Somebody in a public-house shouted at him through the window, 'Come in, fat pig!' Robinson took to his heels.

The town of Stymouth itself is clean,

pleasant, picturesque and well behaved (always excepting the harbour); but it is extremely steep downhill. If Robinson had started one of Aunt Dorcas's eggs rolling at the top of High Street, it would have rolled all the way down to the

bottom; only it would have got broken certainly against a doorstep, or underfoot. There were crowds in the streets as it was market day.

Indeed, it was difficult to walk about without being pushed off the pavement; every old woman that Robinson met seemed to have a basket as big as his own. In the roadway were fish barrows, apple barrows, stalls with crockery and hardware, cocks and hens riding in pony carts, donkeys with panniers and farmers with waggonloads of hay. Also there was a constant string of coal carts coming up from the docks. To a country-bred pig, the noise was confusing and fearful.

Robinson kept his head very creditably until he got into Fore Street, where a

The Tale of Little Pig Robinson

drover's dog was trying to turn three bullocks into a yard, assisted by Stumpy and half the other dogs of the town. Robinson and two other little pigs with baskets of asparagus bolted down an alley and hid in a doorway until the noise of bellowing and barking had passed.

When Robinson took courage to come out again into Fore Street, he decided to follow close behind the tail of a donkey who was carrying panniers piled high with spring broccoli. There was no difficulty in guessing which road led to market. But after all these delays it was not surprising that the church clock struck eleven.

Although it had been open since ten, there were still plenty of customers buying, and wanting to buy, in the market hall. It was a large, airy, light, cheerful, covered-in place, with glass in the roof. It was crowded, but safe and pleasant, compared with the jostling and racket

outside in the cobble-paved streets; at all events there was no risk of being run over. There was a loud hum of voices; market folk cried their wares; customers elbowed and pushed round the stalls. Dairy produce, vegetables, fish and shellfish were displayed upon the flat boards on trestles.

Robinson had found a standing place at one end of a stall where Nanny Netti-goat was selling periwinkles.

'Winkle, winkle! Wink, wink, wink! Maa, maa-a!' bleated Nanny.

Winkles were the only thing that she offered for sale, so she felt no jealousy of Robinson's eggs and primroses. She knew nothing about his cauliflowers; he had the sense to keep them in the basket under the table. He stood on an empty box, quite proud and bold behind the trestle table, singing: 'Eggs, new laid! Fresh new-laid eggs! Who'll come and buy my eggs and daffodillies?'

'I will, sure,' said a large brown dog

with a stumpy tail, 'I'll buy a dozen. My Miss Rose has sent me to market on purpose to buy eggs and butter.'

'I am so sorry, I have no butter, Mr Stumpy; but I have beautiful cauliflowers,' said Robinson, lifting up the basket, after a cautious glance round at Nanny Nettigoat, who might have tried to nibble them. She was busy measuring periwinkles in a pewter mug for a duck customer in a tam-o'-shanter cap. 'They are lovely brown eggs, except one that got cracked; I think that white pussycat at the opposite stall is selling butter – they are beautiful cauliflowers.'

'I'll buy a cauliflower, lovey, bless his little turned-up nose; did he grow them in his own garden?' said old Betsy, bustling up; her rheumatism was better; she had left Susan to keep house. 'No, lovey, I don't want any eggs; I keep hens myself. A cauliflower and a bunch of daffodils for a bow-pot, please,' said Betsy.

'Wee, wee, wee!' replied Robinson.

'Here, Mrs Perkins, come here! Look at this little pig stuck up at a stall all by himself!'

'Well, I don't know!' exclaimed Mrs Perkins, pushing through the crowd, followed by two little girls. 'Well, I never! Are they quite new laid, sonny? Won't go off pop and spoil my Sunday dress like the eggs Mrs Wyandotte took first prize with at five flower shows, till they popped and spoiled the judge's black-silk dress? Not duck eggs, stained with coffee?

That's another trick of flower shows!
New laid, guaranteed? Only you say one
is cracked? Now I call that real honest:
it's no worse for frying. I'll have the dozen
eggs and a cauliflower, please. Look,
Sarah Polly! Look at his silver nose-ring.'

Sarah Polly and her little girl friend
went into fits of giggling, so that

Robinson blushed. He was so confused that he did not notice a lady who wanted to buy his last cauliflower, till she touched him. There was nothing else left to sell, but a bunch of primroses. After more giggling and some whispering the two little girls came back, and bought the primroses. They gave him a peppermint, as well as the penny, which Robinson accepted; but without enthusiasm and with a preoccupied manner.

The trouble was that no sooner had he parted with the bunch of primroses than he realised that he had also sold Aunt Porcas's pattern of darning-wool. He wondered if he ought to ask for it back; but Mrs Perkins and Sarah Polly and her little girl friend had disappeared.

Robinson, having sold everything, came out of the market hall, sucking the peppermint. There were still numbers of people coming in. As Robinson came out upon the steps his basket got caught in the shawl of an elderly sheep, who was pushing her way up. While Robinson was disentangling it, Stumpy came out. He had finished his marketing. His basket was full of heavy purchases. A responsible, trustworthy, obliging dog was Stumpy, glad to do a kindness to anybody.

When Robinson asked him the way to Mr Mumby's, Stumpy said: 'I am going home by Broad Street. Come with me, and I will show you.'

'Wee, wee, wee! Oh, thank you, Stumpy!' said Robinson.

Chapter 5

Old Mr Mumby was a deaf old man in spectacles who kept a general store. He sold almost anything you can imagine, except ham — a circumstance much approved by Aunt Dorcas. It was the only general store in Stymouth where you would not find displayed upon the counter a large dish containing strings of thin, pale-coloured, repulsively uncooked sausages, and see rolled bacon hanging from the ceiling.

'What pleasure,' said Aunt Dorcas feelingly — 'what possible pleasure can there be in entering a shop where you knock your head against a ham? A ham that may have belonged to a dear second cousin?'

Therefore the aunts bought their sugar and tea, their blue bag, their soap, their frying pans, matches and mugs from old Mr Mumby.

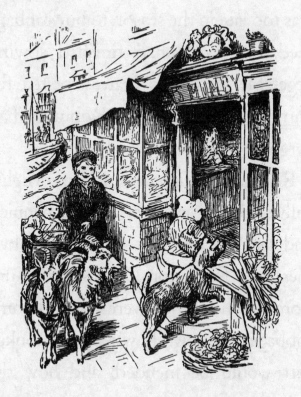

All these things he sold, and many more besides, and what he did not keep in stock he would obtain to order. But as yeast requires to be quite fresh, he did not sell it; he advised Robinson to ask for yeast at a baker's shop. Also he said it was too late in the season to buy cabbage seed; everybody had finished sowing vegetable seeds this year. Worsted for darning he did sell; but Robinson had forgotten the colour.

Robinson bought six sticks of delightfully sticky barley sugar with his pennies, and listened carefully to Mr Mumby's messages for Aunt Dorcas and Aunt Porcas — how they were to send some cabbages next week when the donkey cart would be mended; and how the kettle was not repaired yet; and there was a new patent box-iron he would like to recommend to Aunt Porcas.

Robinson said, 'Wee, wee, wee?' and listened, and little dog Tipkins, who stood on a stool behind the counter, tying up grocery parcels in blue paper bags — little dog Tipkins whispered to Robinson — 'Were there any rats this spring in the barn at Piggery Porcombe? And what would Robinson be doing on Saturday afternoon?'

'Wee, wee, wee!' answered Robinson.

Robinson came out of Mr Mumby's, heavily laden. The barley sugar was comforting; but he was troubled about the darning wool, the yeast, and the cabbage seed. He was looking about rather anxiously when again he met old Betsy, who exclaimed: 'Bless the little piggy! Not gone home yet? Now it must not stop in Stymouth till it gets its pocket picked!'

Robinson explained his difficulty about the darning-wool.

Kind old Betsy was ready with help.

'Why, I noticed the wool round the little primrose posy; it was a blue-grey colour like the last pair of socks that I knitted for Sam. Come with me to the wool shop – Fleecy Flock's wool shop. I remember the colour; well I do!' said Betsy.

Mrs Flock was the sheep that had run against Robinson; she had bought herself three turnips and come straight

The Tale of Little Pig Robinson

home from market for fear of missing customers while her shop was locked up.

Such a shop! Such a jumble! Wool in all sorts of colours, thick wool, thin wool, fingering wool and rug wool, bundles and bundles all jumbled up; and she could not put her hoof on anything. She was so confused and slow at finding things that Betsy got impatient.

'No, I don't want wool for slippers; darning-wool, Fleecy; *darning wool*, same colour as I bought for my Sam's socks. Bless me, *no*, not knitting needles! Darning wool.'

'Baa, baa! Did you say white or black, m'm? Three ply, was it?'

'Oh, dear me, *grey* darning-wool on cards; not heather mixture.'

'I know I have it somewhere,' said Fleecy Flock helplessly, jumbling up the skeins and bundles. 'Sim Ram came in this morning with part of the Ewehampton clip; my shop is completely cluttered up – '

It took half an hour to find the wool. If Betsy had not been with him, Robinson never would have got it.

'It's that late, I must go home,' said Betsy. 'My Sam is on shore today for dinner. If you take my advice you will leave that big heavy basket with the Miss Goldfinches, and hurry with your shopping. It's a long uphill walk home to Piggery Porcombe.'

Robinson, anxious to follow old Betsy's advice, walked towards the Miss Goldfinches. On the way he came to a baker's, and he remembered the yeast.

It was not the right sort of baker's, unfortunately. There was a nice bakery smell, and pastry in the window; but it was an eating house or cook shop.

When he pushed the swing door open, a man in an apron and a square white cap turned round and said, 'Hello! Is this a pork pie walking on its hind legs? — and four rude men at a dining-table burst out laughing.

Robinson left the shop in a hurry. He felt afraid to go into any other baker's shop. He was looking wistfully into another window in Fore Street when Stumpy saw him again. He had taken his own basket home, and come out on another errand. He carried Robinson's basket in his mouth and took him to a very safe baker's, where he was accustomed to buy dog biscuits for himself. There Robinson purchased Aunt Dorcas's yeast at last.

They searched in vain for cabbage seed; they were told that the only likely place was a little store on the quay, kept by a pair of wagtails.

'It is a pity I cannot go with you,' said Stumpy. 'My Miss Rose has sprained her ankle; she sent me to fetch twelve postage stamps, and I must take them home to her before the post goes out. Do not try to carry this heavy basket down and up the steps; leave it with the Miss Goldfinches.'

Robinson was very grateful to Stumpy. The two Miss Goldfinches kept a tea and coffee tavern which was patronised by Aunt Dorcas and the quieter market people. Over the door was a signboard upon which was painted a fat little green bird called 'The Contented Siskin', which was the name of their coffee tavern. They had a stable where the carrier's donkey rested when he came into Stymouth with the washing on Saturdays.

Robinson looked so tired that the elder Miss Goldfinch gave him a cup of tea; but they both told him to drink it up quickly.

'Wee, wee, wee! Yock, yock!' said Robinson, scalding his nose.

In spite of their respect for Aunt Dorcas, the Miss Goldfinches disapproved of his solitary shopping; and they said that the basket was far too heavy for him.

'Neither of us could lift it,' said the elder Miss Goldfinch, holding out a tiny claw. 'Get your cabbage seed and hurry back. Sim Ram's pony gig is still waiting in our stable. If you come back before he starts I feel sure he will give you a lift; at all events he will make room for your basket under the seat – and he passes Piggery Porcombe. Run away now!'

'Wee, wee, wee!' said Robinson.

'Whatever were they thinking of to let him come alone? He will never get home before dark,' said the elder Miss Goldfinch. 'Fly to the stable, Clara; tell Sim Ram's pony not to start without the basket.'

The younger Miss Goldfinch flew across the yard. They were industrious, sprightly little lady birds, who kept lump sugar and thistle seed as well as tea in their tea-caddies. Their tables and china were spotlessly clean.

Chapter 6

Stymouth was full of inns; too full. The farmers usually put up their horses at the Black Bull or the Horse and Farrier; the smaller market people patronised the Pig and Whistle.

There was another inn called the Crown and Anchor at the corner of Fore Street. It was much frequented by seamen; several were lounging about the door with their hands in their pockets. One sailor-man in a blue jersey sauntered across the road, staring very hard at Robinson.

Said he — 'I say, little pig! do you like snuff?'

Now if Robinson had a fault, it was

that he could not say no; not even to a hedgehog stealing eggs. As a matter of fact, snuff or tobacco made him sick. But instead of saying, 'No, thank you, Mr Man,' and going straight away about his business, he shuffled his feet, half closed one eye, hung his head on one side and grunted.

The sailor pulled out a horn snuff box and presented a small pinch to Robinson, who wrapped it up in a little bit of paper, intending to give it to Aunt Dorcas. Then, not to be outdone in politeness, he offered the sailor-man some barley sugar.

If Robinson was not fond of snuff, at all events his new acquaintance had no objection to candy. He ate an alarming

quantity. Then he pulled Robinson's ear and complimented him, and said he had five chins. He promised to take Robinson to the cabbage-seed shop; and, finally, he begged to have the honour of showing him over a ship engaged in the ginger trade, commanded by Captain Barnabas Butcher and named the *Pound of Candles*.

Robinson did not very much like the name. It reminded him of tallow, of lard, of crackle and trimmings of bacon. But he allowed himself to be led away, smiling shyly and walking on his toes. If Robinson had only known . . . that man was a ship's cook!

As they turned down the steep narrow lane leading out of High Street to the harbour, old Mr Mumby at his shop door called out anxiously, 'Robinson! Robinson!' But there was too much noise of carts. And a customer coming into the shop at that moment distracted his attention and he forgot the suspicious behaviour of the sailor. Otherwise, out of regard for the family, he would undoubtedly have ordered his dog, Tipkins, to go and fetch Robinson back. As it was, he was the first person to give useful information to the police when Robinson had been missed. But it was then too late.

Robinson and his new friend went down the long flight of steps to the harbour basin — very high steps, steep and slippery. The little pig was obliged to jump from step to step until the sailor kindly took hold of him. They walked along the quay hand in hand: their appearance seemed to cause unbounded amusement.

Robinson looked about him with much interest. He had peeped over those steps before when he had come into Stymouth in the donkey cart, but he had never ventured to go down, because the sailors are rather rough and because they frequently have little snarling terriers on guard about their vessels.

There were ever so many ships in the harbour; the noise and bustle was almost as loud as it had been up above in the market square. A big three-masted ship called the *Goldilocks* was discharging a cargo of oranges; and farther along the quay, a small coasting brig called *Little Bo Peep* of Bristol was loading up with bales of wool belonging to the sheep of Ewehampton and Lambworthy.

Old Sim Ram, with a sheep bell and big curly horns, stood by the gangway keeping count of the bales. Every time the crane swung round and let down another bale of wool into the hold, with

a scuffle of rope through the pulley,
Simon Ram nodded his old head, and
the bell went 'tinkle, tinkle, tong', and he
gave a gruff bleat.

He was a person who knew Robinson
by sight and ought to have warned him.
He had often passed Piggery Porcombe
when he drove down the lane in his
gig. But his blind eye was turned towards
the quay; and he had been flustered
and confused by an argument with the
pursers as to whether thirty-five bales of
wool had been hoisted on board already
or only thirty-four.

So he kept his one useful eye carefully
on the wool, and counted it by the
notches on his tally stick – another bale –
another notch – thirty-five, thirty-six,

thirty-seven; he hoped the number would come right at the finish.

His bob-tailed sheep dog, Timothy Gyp, was also acquainted with Robinson, but he was busy superintending a dog fight between an Airedale terrier belonging to the collier *Margery Daw* and a Spanish dog belonging to the *Goldilocks*. No one took any notice of their growling and snarling, which ended in both rolling over the side of the quay and falling into the water. Robinson kept close to the sailor and held his hand very tight.

The *Pound of Candles* proved to be a good-sized schooner, newly painted and decorated with certain flags, whose significance was not understood by Robinson. She lay near the outer end of the jetty. The tide was running up fast, lapping against the ship's sides and straining the thick hawsers by which she was moored to the quay.

The crew were stowing goods on board and doing things with ropes under the direction of Captain Barnabas Butcher, a lean, brown, nautical person with a rasping voice. He banged things about and grumbled; parts of his remarks were audible on the quay. He was speaking about the tug *Sea Horse* — and about the spring tide, with a north-east wind behind it — and the baker's man and fresh vegetables — 'to be shipped at eleven sharp; likewise a joint of . . . ' He stopped short suddenly, and his eye lighted upon the cook and Robinson.

The Tale of Little Pig Robinson

Robinson and the cook went on board across a shaky plank. When Robinson stepped on to the deck, he found himself face to face with a large yellow cat who was blacking boots.

The cat gave a start of surprise and

dropped its blacking brush. It then began to wink and make extraordinary faces at Robinson. He had never seen a cat behave in that way before. He enquired whether it was ill. Whereupon the cook threw a boot at it and it rushed up into the rigging. But Robinson he invited most affably to descend into the cabin, to partake of muffins and crumpets.

I do not know how many muffins Robinson consumed. He went on eating them until he fell asleep; and he went on sleeping until his stool gave a lurch and he fell off and rolled under the table. One side of the cabin floor swung up to the ceiling; and the other side of the ceiling swung down to the floor. Plates danced about; and there were shoutings and thumpings and rattling of chains and other bad sounds.

Robinson picked himself up, feeling bumped. He scrambled up a sort of a ladder-staircase on to the deck. Then he gave squeal upon squeal of horror! All round the ship there were great big green waves; the houses on the quay were like dolls' houses; and high up inland, above the red cliffs and green fields, he could see the farm of Piggery Porcombe looking no bigger than a postage stamp. A little white patch in the orchard was Aunt Porcas's washing, spread out to bleach upon the grass. Near at hand the black tug *Sea Horse* smoked and plunged and rolled. They were winding in the tow rope which had just been cast loose from the *Pound of Candles*.

Captain Barnabas stood up in the bows of his schooner; he yelled and shouted to the master of the tug. The sailors shouted also, and pulled with a will, and hoisted the sails. The ship heeled over and rushed through the waves, and there was a smell of the sea.

As for Robinson – he tore round and round the deck like one distracted, shrieking very shrill and loud. Once or twice he slipped down, for the deck was extremely sideways; but still he ran and he ran. Gradually his squeals subsided into singing, but still he kept on running, and this is what he sang —

'Poor pig Robinson Crusoe!
Oh, how in the world could they do so?
They have set him afloat, in a horrible boat,
Oh, poor pig Robinson Crusoe!'

The sailors laughed until they cried; but when Robinson had sung that same verse about fifty times, and upset several sailors by rushing between their legs, they began to get angry. Even the ship's cook was no longer civil to Robinson. On the contrary, he was very rude indeed. He said that if Robinson did not leave off singing through his nose, he would make him into pork chops.

Then Robinson fainted, and fell flat upon the deck of the *Pound of Candles*.

Chapter 7

It must not be supposed for one moment that Robinson was ill-treated on board ship. Quite the contrary. He was even better fed and more petted on the *Pound of Candles* than he had been at Piggery Porcombe. So, after a few days' fretting for his kind old aunts (especially while he was seasick), Robinson became perfectly contented and happy. He found what is called his 'sea legs'; and he scampered about the deck until the time when he became too fat and lazy to scamper.

The cook was never tired of boiling porridge for him. A whole sackful of meal and a sack of potatoes appeared to have been provided especially for his benefit and pleasure. He could eat as much as he pleased. It pleased him to eat a great deal and to lie on the warm boards of the deck. He got lazier and lazier as the ship sailed south into warmer weather. The mate made a pet of him; the crew gave him tit-bits. The cook rubbed his back and scratched his sides — his ribs could not be tickled, because he had laid so much fat on. The only persons who refused to treat him as a joke were the yellow tom-cat and Captain Barnabas Butcher, who was of a sour disposition.

The attitude of the cat was perplexing to Robinson. Obviously it disapproved

The Tale of Little Pig Robinson

of the maize-meal porridge business, and it spoke mysteriously about the impropriety of greediness and about the disastrous results of over indulgence. But it did not explain what those results might be, and as the cat itself cared neither for yellow meal nor 'taties, Robinson thought that its warnings might arise from prejudice. It was not unfriendly. It was mournful and foreboding.

The cat itself was crossed in love. Its morose and gloomy outlook upon life was partly the result of separation from the owl. That sweet hen-bird, a snowy owl of Lapland, had sailed upon a northern whaler, bound for Greenland. Whereas the *Pound of Candles* was heading for the tropic seas.

Therefore the cat neglected its duties, and was upon the worst of terms with the cook. Instead of blacking boots and valeting the captain, it spent days and nights in the rigging, serenading the moon. Between times it came down on deck and remonstrated with Robinson.

It never told him plainly why he ought not to eat so much; but it referred frequently to a mysterious date (which

Robinson could never remember) – the date of Captain Butcher's birthday, which he celebrated annually by an extra good dinner.

'That's what they are saving up apples for. The onions are done – sprouted with the heat. I heard Captain Barnabas tell the cook that onions were of no consequence as long as there were apples for sauce.'

Robinson paid no attention. In fact, he and the cat were both on the side of the ship, watching a shoal of silvery fishes. The ship was completely becalmed. The cook strolled across the deck to see what the cat was looking at and exclaimed joyfully at the sight of fresh fish. Presently half the crew were

fishing. They baited their lines with bits of scarlet wool and bits of biscuit; and the boatswain had a successful catch on a line baited with a shiny button.

The worst of button fishing was that so many fish dropped off while being hauled on deck. Consequently Captain Butcher allowed the crew to launch the jolly boat, which was let down from some iron contraption called 'the davits' on to the glassy surface of the sea. Five sailors got into the boat; the cat jumped in also. They fished for hours. There was not a breath of wind.

In the absence of the cat, Robinson fell asleep peacefully upon the warm deck. Later he was disturbed by the voices of the mate and the cook, who had not gone fishing.

The former was saying: 'I don't fancy loin of pork with sunstroke, cooky. Stir him up; or else throw a piece of sailcloth over him. I was bred on a farm myself. Pigs should never be let sleep in a hot sun.'

'As why?' enquired the cook.

'Sunstroke,' replied the mate. 'Likewise it scorches the skin; makes it peely like; spoils the look of the crackling.'

At this point a rather heavy dirty piece of sailcloth was flung over Robinson, who struggled and kicked with sudden grunts.

'Did he hear you, matey?' asked the cook in a lower voice.

'Don't know; don't matter; he can't get off the ship,' replied the mate, lighting his pipe.

'Might upset his appetite; he's feeding beautiful,' said the cook.

Presently the voice of Captain Barnabas Butcher was heard. He had come up on deck after a siesta below in his cabin.

'Proceed to the crow's nest on the main mast; observe the horizon through a telescope according to latitude and longitude. We ought to be among the archipelago by the chart and compass,' said the voice of Captain Butcher.

It reached the ears of Robinson through the sailcloth in muffled tones, but peremptory; although it was not so received by the mate, who occasionally contradicted the captain when no one else was listening.

'My corns are very painful,' said the mate.

'Send the cat up,' ordered Captain Barnabas briefly.

'The cat is out in the boat fishing.'

'Fetch him in then,' said Captain

Barnabas, losing his temper. 'The rascal has not blacked my boots for a fortnight.' He then went below; that is, down a step-ladder into his cabin, where he proceeded to work out the latitude and longitude again, in search of the archipelago.

'It's to be hoped that he mends his temper before next Thursday, or he won't enjoy roast pork!' said the mate to the cook.

They strolled to the other end of the deck to see what fish had been caught; the boat was coming back.

As the weather was perfectly calm, it was left overnight upon the glassy sea, tied below a porthole at the stern of the *Pound of Candles*.

The cat was sent up the mast with a

telescope; it remained there for some time. When it came down it reported quite untruthfully that there was nothing in sight. No particular watch or lookout was kept that night upon the *Pound of Candles* because the ocean was so calm. The cat was supposed to watch — if anybody did. All the rest of the ship's company played cards.

Not so the cat or Robinson. The cat had noticed a slight movement under the sailcloth. It found Robinson shivering with fright and in floods of tears. He had overheard the conversation about pork.

'I'm sure I have given you enough hints,' said the cat to Robinson. 'What do you suppose they were feeding you

up for? Now don't start squealing, you
little fool! It's as easy as snuff, if you will
listen and stop crying. You can row,
after a fashion.' (Robinson had been out
fishing occasionally and caught several
crabs.) 'Well, you have not far to go;

I could see the top of the bong tree on an island to the north-east when I was up the mast. The straits of the archipelago are too shallow for the *Pound of Candles*, and I'll scuttle all the other boats. Come along, and do what I tell you!' said the cat.

The cat, actuated partly by unselfish friendship and partly by a grudge against the cook and Captain Barnabas Butcher, assisted Robinson to collect a varied assortment of necessaries. Shoes, sealing-wax, a knife, an armchair, fishing tackle, a straw hat, a saw, fly papers, a potato pot, a telescope, a kettle, a compass, a hammer, a barrel of flour, another of meal, a keg of fresh water, a tumbler, a teapot, nails, a bucket, a screwdriver —

'That reminds me,' said the cat, and what did it do but go round the deck with a gimlet and bore large holes in the three boats that remained on board the *Pound of Candles*.

By this time there began to be ominous sounds below; those of the sailors who had had bad hands were beginning to be tired of carding. So the cat took a hasty farewell of Robinson, pushed him over the ship's side and helped him slide down the rope into the boat. The cat unfastened the upper end of the rope and threw it after him. Then it ascended the rigging and pretended to sleep upon its watch.

Robinson stumbled somewhat in taking his seat at the oars. His legs were

short for rowing. Captain Barnabas in
the cabin suspended his deal, a card in
his hand, listening (the cook took the
opportunity to look under the card),
then he went on slapping down the cards,
which drowned the sound of oars upon
the placid sea.

After another hand, two sailors left the cabin and went on deck. They noticed something having the appearance of a large black beetle in the distance. One of them said it was an enormous

cockroach, swimming with its hind legs. The other said it was a dolphinium. They disputed, rather loudly. Captain Barnabas, who had had a hand with no trumps at all after the cook's dealing — Captain Barnabas came on deck and said: 'Bring me my telescope.'

The telescope had disappeared; likewise the shoes, the sealing-wax, the compass, the potato pot, the straw hat, the hammer, the nails, the bucket, the screwdriver and the armchair.

'Take the jolly boat and see what it is,' ordered Captain Butcher.

'All jolly fine, but suppose it is a dolphinium?' said the mate mutinously.

'Why, bless my life, the jolly boat is gone!' exclaimed a sailor.

'Take another boat, take all the three other boats; it's that pig and that cat!' roared the captain.

'Nay, sir, the cat's up the rigging asleep.'

'Bother the cat! Get the pig back! The apple sauce will be wasted!' shrieked the cook, dancing about and brandishing a knife and fork.

The davits were swung out, the boats were let down with a swish and a splash, all the sailors tumbled in, and rowed frantically. And most of them were glad to row frantically back to the *Pound of Candles*. For every boat leaked badly, thanks to the cat.

Chapter 8

Robinson rowed away from the *Pound of Candles.* He tugged steadily at the oars. They were heavy for him. The sun had set, but I understand that in the tropics – I have never been there – there is a phosphorescent light upon the sea. When Robinson lifted his oars, the sparkling water dripped from the blades like diamonds. And presently the moon began to rise above the horizon – rising like half a great silver plate. Robinson rested on his oars and gazed at the ship, motionless in the moonlight, on a sea without a ripple. It was at this moment – he being a quarter of a mile away – that the two sailors came on deck, and thought his boat was a swimming beetle.

Robinson was too far away to see or hear the uproar on board the *Pound of Candles*; but he did presently perceive that three boats were starting in pursuit. Involuntarily he commenced to squeal, and rowed frantically. But before he had time to exhaust himself by racing, the ship's boats turned back. Then Robinson remembered the cat's work with the gimlet, and he knew that the boats were leaking. For the rest of the night he rowed quietly, without haste. He was not inclined to sleep, and the air was pleasantly cool. Next day it was hot, but Robinson slept soundly under the sailcloth, which the cat had been careful to send with him, in case he wished to rig up a tent.

The ship receded from view – you know the sea is not really flat. First he could not see the hull, then he could not see the deck, then only part of the masts, then nothing at all.

Robinson had been steering his course by the ship. Having lost sight of this direction sign, he turned round to consult his compass — when bump, bump, the boat touched a sandbank. Fortunately it did not stick.

Robinson stood up in the boat, working one oar backwards and gazing around. What should he see but the top of the bong tree!

Half an hour's rowing brought him to the beach of a large and fertile island. He landed in the most approved manner in a convenient sheltered bay, where a stream of boiling water flowed down the silvery strand. The shore was covered with oysters. Acid drops and sweets grew upon the trees. Yams, which are a sort of sweet potato, abounded ready cooked. The bread-fruit tree grew iced cakes and muffins, ready baked; so no pig need sigh for porridge. Overhead towered the bong tree.

If you want a more detailed description of the island, you must read *Robinson Crusoe*. The island of the bong tree was very like Crusoe's, only without its drawbacks. I have never been there myself, so I rely upon the report of the owl and the pussycat, who visited it eighteen months later, and spent a delightful honeymoon there. They spoke enthusiastically about the climate – only it was a little too warm for the owl.

Later on Robinson was visited by Stumpy and little dog Tipkins. They found him perfectly contented, and in the best of good health. He was not at all inclined to return to Stymouth. For anything I know he may be living there still upon the island. He grew fatter and fatter and more fatterer; and the ship's cook never found him.

Cecily Parsley's Nursery Rhymes

For Little Peter in New Zealand

Cecily Parsley lived in a pen,
And brewed good ale for gentlemen;

Beatrix Potter

Gentlemen came every day,
Till Cecily Parsley ran away.

Cecily Parsley's Nursery-Rhymes

Goosey, goosey, gander,
Whither will you wander?
Upstairs and downstairs,
And in my lady's chamber!

Beatrix Potter

This pig went to market;
This pig stayed at home;

This pig had a bit of meat;

And this pig had none;

This little pig cried,
 'Wee! wee! wee!
I can't find my way home.'

Beatrix Potter

Pussycat sits by the fire;
How should she be fair?
In walks the little dog,
Says, 'Pussy! are you there?'

Cecily Parsley's Nursery-Rhymes

'How do you do, Mistress Pussy?
 Mistress Pussy, how do you do?'
'I thank you kindly, little dog,
 I fare as well as you!'

Beatrix Potter

Three blind mice, three blind mice,
  See how they run!
They all run after the farmer's wife,
And she cut off their tails with a
                    carving knife!
Did you ever see such a thing in
                    your life
  As three blind mice?

'Bow, wow, wow!'
　　Whose dog art thou?
'I'm little Tom Tinker's dog,
　　Bow, wow, wow!'

Beatrix Potter

We have a little garden,
  A garden of our own,
And every day we water there
  The seeds that we have sown.

Cecily Parsley's Nursery-Rhymes

We love our little garden,
    And tend it with such care,
You will not find a faded leaf
    Or blighted blossom there.

Beatrix Potter

Ninny nanny netticoat,
In a white petticoat,
    With a red nose –
The longer she stands,
    The shorter she grows.